NALA - BOOK OF LAW

PREQUEL IN PANTHEON

SARALYN EVERHART

TAYLOR BROCKWAY

CONTENTS

To my crazy beautiful wife, my knight in shining armor, my Nala, thank you for always being sword-ready to fight my battles.

CONTENT WARNING

As much as I appreciate you being here, please be advised this book contains mature topics that may not be suitable for all audiences. Scenes may include extreme violence, anxiety, abuse, gambling, animal abuse, murder, coercion, mentions of enslaved people, war, and death.
Take care of yourself and your mental health, above all, before reading.
You are in charge of your peace.

"In the face of death, justice is the final testament that transcends mortal reality, ensuring fairness prevails even in your last breath."

- *Clockwork* from NALA: *Book of Law*

THE CITY OF BRAYER
THE DWARVEN KINGDOM
THORBURN
THE MORT
THROTH
HIDDEN CITY OF MER-FOLK

L REALM

OSSROADS
BLACK DRAGON ISLE

THE GRAND ORC ENCLAVE
THE FORBIDDEN FOREST
MOUNTAINSIDE
SEA OF DREAD
PALADIN SCHOOL
DARKNESS INCARNATE
N
W E
S
0 5 10 15 20
THE ELVEN KINGDOM

PROLOGUE

WHO ARE YOU?

When he materializes the blue aura of Aeo's soul pulses, enveloping the space and caressing it like a delicate hand.

"Nala Delvimir. Baalthor's prodigy Paladin. What morals do you follow that lead you to being Baalthor's champion? It could not possibly be just hatred."

"If you are the father of this universe, you should know these answers. I am a follower of vengeance. When a debt is to be paid, I ensure it is fulfilled."

"That explains why you and Baalthor get along, but it doesn't explain your goals. What are you trying to make of yourself?"

"I want the rights righted and the wrongs dealt with. I don't want my people to be afraid anymore."

His color shifts. Not to anything angry, but to yellow. The color of understanding. "You are mediocre, and yet, Clockwork saved your life. Whatever you stand for, Nala, let it make this world greater than I left it."

"I stand for a world where Romar is dead. That is justice enough for everything he took part in."

"Nala Delvimir. I know which domain fits you the best." His color returns to blue, and he chuckles beneath a breath. A book bound in gold appears with a snap beyond his glow. Falling into my hands, the cover glows.

"I don't understand. What about my trials?"

He is gone when I look for him, the white world falling from my eyes.

CHAPTER 1

ALL IS FAIR

I had to kill my soulmate.

Rubbing my eyes, I tried to remove her name beneath mine, but it was inked. It was official. We were both placed in the same college.

War.

Students brushed against my shoulders, pushing me aside to check for their names.

There were five colleges. Out of five Paladin colleges, the headmaster had to choose the same for both of us.

Was it fate?

The room buzzed beneath the noise of chattering students. Booths were set up and lines were forming. I should be finding my place, but Echo is late. Late and ignorant of this knowledge, I'm sure.

The Paladins of War go head to head in their senior semester: the last one standing graduates. One of us will die.

Her black scales beamed in the light and Echo shoved through to meet me, panting from her run. "Nala."

We were the only Dragonkin from Black Dragon Isle to

graduate from the junior academy. Our classmates consisted of humans and elves, with scarce chromatic dragonkin among us. Leaving behind our friends to choose new paths, we stood at the top of our class. It should not be this much of a surprise. We were paired in the College of War because of our strength.

Wrapping her in a short embrace, I dropped my smile. "We were paired together."

"Which college?" She stood on her toes, looking across heads to see the corkboard.

I held my breath. "War."

"War?" she lowered her heels, water gathering in her eyes. "Of all choices..."

"I know."

"We will demand a displacement."

"Echo."

She turned, looking for the headmaster. "He will be understanding. You are just as smart as you are good with a sword. You will do well in Pride or Power."

"Echo." I sighed, reaching for her arm.

Spinning to grip me by the shoulders, she shook her head. "No. I do not accept this."

Our eyes danced with each other. She knew this was non-negotiable.

I dropped my voice into a whisper, my gaze hitting the floor. "Echo."

Echo had been my best friend for as long as I could remember, from neighbors to schoolmates. And now, soon-to-be opponents against death.

Her eyes darted across the room, searching for anyone to fix this mistake. But the headmaster wrote this list and we both knew he would not change it. As the top students at junior paladin school, there was never any doubt we would be competing. We didn't want to think about it in the early days. After all, this is why you don't befriend your classmates in Paladin School.

Power above pleasure and respect above equality. That is how you win.

The chilled kiss of her scales pressed against mine as I gripped her arm. She returned her sad gaze, but we strode toward the booth marked as the Church of War together. Banners of red and black wrapped around the table and hung from the ceiling above. With a short line, a couple of students stood before us, shifting their feet and picking at their skin.

A human girl, no older than fifteen. An orcish man, confidence in his straightened spine.

They were walking corpses, waiting for time to wash them away beneath the success of others.

Shouting enveloped the unease and we all turned to watch a man and woman reunite in front of the Church of Strategy. My heart sank.

They would live. Whether their relationship did or not, they wouldn't have to kill each other to graduate. My gaze darted across the rest of the students piled into lines.

With black leather and short swords, the line to the Church of Evil was the longest. The Church of Pride followed second, full of mostly men.

No surprise there.

Then there was the Church of Power—the shortest line of them all. The Church of Power had strict criteria for students to be enrolled in their curriculum. More stringent than War.

Echo brushed her shoulder against mine, nodding forward. I returned to face the man behind the table. His ears pointed out from behind his dark hair. When he raised a brow expectantly, a scar running vertically down his face stretched. "Name?"

"Nala Delvimir."

Short of any emotion, his eyes fell to a scroll in his grasp, and he searched for my name. He crossed it off when he found it and sorted through envelopes. "Your room key, class schedule, and other enrollment documents will be here."

Stamped on the front of it was Baalthor's divine symbol, and it sank into my gaze as I realized what this meant to me. Thankful that Echo stood behind me, I let my lips curl into a prideful smirk as the envelope chilled at my touch.

I was going to be a Paladin of War.

A soldier of Baalthor.

A Champion.

Standing there longer than necessary, I had forgotten to move, and his eyes moved past mine. "Name?"

"Echo Riftwood."

Guilt settled where that pride was building in my stomach, and I remembered my surroundings. She stepped forward as her name was crossed off, taking her envelope as she joined my side again. We stayed silent, grieving. Death gripped us both by the necks. But we couldn't yield to one another. Paladins of the Church of War did not relent. And even though we knew one of us would die by the other's hand, until the end, we vowed to pretend that day would never come.

"Ms. Delvimir."

The bite of a chill ran through my spine as I turned to greet the voice behind us. "Headmaster Biron."

Towering the two of us was Biron's half-dragon form. It gleamed, his teeth sticking out from his smirk. "I hope you are as proud as I am. You were selected into one of the best colleges. I see you leading armies one day in Baalthor's armies. From speaking highly of you, he already knows your name."

Baalthor, knows my name?

"I cannot thank you enough for this opportunity."

Echo scoffed, and the headmaster turned to glare at her. "Do you have a problem?"

"N-No, sir." She backtracked, eyes wide.

"I understand the two of you are supposed to be close friends. Unfortunately, these types of education require sacrifice. I hope you enjoy your time together while it lasts, but do not let it hold you back from excelling. You both scored high on your test results last semester. As a top student, I have high expectations."

Straightening his back, he looked behind him at a calling voice.

"Headmaster."

"It seems I am needed elsewhere. I will talk with you ladies later one-on-one. Do not forget what we talked about." His eyes locked with mine.

I nodded, and he waded through the crowd to where somebody needed him, the gleam of his sword tapping his hip.

"Can you believe him?" With distance in her eyes, Echo stared daggers at where he walked away. "Placing us in the same college and expecting us to turn on each other?"

"What are we going to do about it, Echo?"

Her throat bobbed, and she quieted.

There was nothing we could do about it.

"I-I..."

"I am going to go check in at the dormitory. Let me

know when you figure it out." I turned from her, my fist clenched in front of me so she couldn't see.

Despite the worry and sadness, I was excited and ready. I was prepared to serve in Baalthor's armies.

To serve at his side.

And Headmaster Biron knew it.

THE BITTER WINTER CHILL BIT MY SCALES. EVEN A COLD-BLOODED creature such as a dragon couldn't stand the mainland winters. The Isle of Dragons sat twenty miles off the eastern coast. No one flew out that far unless they were searching for it, so it was the perfect location for the dragons to live separately in peace.

Crunching beneath my feet was the grass folding. The cold already froze it. We were expecting snow in the next few days. Shuffling my papers, I searched for the dormitory information and pulled the key from my pocket. The colleges separated everything. Although most students have roommates, the College of War students lived separately due to the risk of being murdered by other students.

All was fair in the College of War.

After all, we were paladin students preparing to join the military for the God of War himself.

With the path separating five brick buildings, each dormitory was decorated with their college's banners. As the red and black banner of war waves in the brisk breeze, I take a breath and continue my stride. Three flights of stairs and a couple of hallways later, the wooden door with the number three hundred and eight stands as my home for the next five months. Then, after I graduate, I will join the church and serve Baalthor.

The room, which was creaking, held a simple hay bed, a wooden dresser, and a desk. The sill of the window was decorated with red curtains, overlooking the courtyard between the dorms and faculty buildings.

My heart sank.

It wasn't going to be me that died here, and everyone knew it. There wasn't a chance I would be beaten by Echo or any other Paladin students for the War College. I had the top scores.

As pride-filling as it was, it meant I would have to kill my classmates to graduate.

The wood floor creaked, but not from my own movement. Dragging my eyes to the door, the irking sound belonged to a shadow cast by outside light, dancing below the door as two feet appeared to stop. Was this it? Had the games begun? If I was to be murdered, would it be in the comfort of my dorm?

It took a single breath to unsheathe my hidden dagger along my belt loop and raise it as I slowly stalked toward the uninvited stranger. They didn't move for several seconds and I snuck closer, preparing for anything except for the knock. A brisk and peppy knock rattles from the other side and a female clears her throat beneath a slight hum.

Blowing a breath and returning the dagger to its sheath, I twist the door open and shake my head at Echo. "Have you gotten to your dorm yet?"

"Well, no, but I did run into my buddy from the College of Power and they are hosting a party tonight. I figured I should tell you before you make any other plans."

"How did you..." I look down the hall, following whispering voices from outside their rooms. "Who told you my room number?"

Curling her eyebrows, she glanced in the direction I looked. "Why? You weren't going to tell me?"

I studied her as long as she looked at me, several breaths too long. "It's not that."

"Really?"

"Everything has changed, Echo. You cannot trust any information from anyone."

"The Room's Advisor." She looks back down the hall. "I'm her neighbor on floor two. It was a favor."

I wasn't concerned *about* Echo. I was concerned *for* Echo. She's trusting and kind. Considering her for the College of War, the headmaster must have lost a few marbles. There was no doubt she could wield a weapon just as well as any soldier, but the gore and regret would ruin her good nature.

And I hated that.

Clearing my throat and breaking the silence, she snapped back to me, that gleam of excitement returning to her eyes. "So, about that party?"

"Yeah, yeah. Come on in." I wave her through my door. "I still have some of my Dragon's Hoard Beauty mois-turizers."

Her eyes sparkle. "Really?"

THE DRAGON RACES HAVE BEEN AT WAR WITH OTHER SPECIES IN humanity since the beginning of documented society. It wasn't a surprise to turn the page of my book and read about the uprising of evil cults among the chromatic-scaled dragon societies. They had a more selfish ideology than the metallic-scaled dragons who preferred to be a democracy.

Shouting curses, a man stumbled back with his drink sloshing from his hand, the contents splattering into my lap and covering my book.

Curling my nose, I throw a hand up. "What the fuck?"

"Oh." With a hand braced on the wall above where I sat on the floor, he glances down with a shocked expression. "Are you reading a book right now?"

"Not anymore." Snapping the soiled book closed, I would have to study later when the pages dry out. My eyes danced around him as I stood, searching for Echo among the crowd. She had promised to grab some drinks thirty minutes ago, but hadn't returned.

The man watched me, unbelieving that I had been slumped against a wall instead of participating in the party Echo had dragged me to. When the lute player stopped and the crowd cheered again, he startled. He returned to dancing his way through people, stumbling and shouting as he went.

Watching his back, I waited until I was sure he would make it past everyone to turn to Echo who was calling me.

"I am so, so sorry that I left you here." She panted. "But I did bring a friend I would love to introduce you to."

The half-orc man she referred to seemed to belong to some high secret society. His hair was slicked back with a shine and his black button-down shirt was well-ironed. He reeked of wealth.

"Echo has spoken highly of you, but of course, so has everyone in the school."

Even his voice irritated my scales.

Noticing my hesitancy, Echo laughed and joined my

side. "This is Morgen. He's number two in the school rank-ing, right between us."

He nods with a half-smile. "What a shame, too. I would've loved to have gotten to know you. But we should make these last few months count anyway."

Echo *actually blushed* at the man. I would've slapped him if he had said that to me. What an asshole.

Morgen turned, noting his name being shouted from behind him. Another man I didn't recognize slapped him and exchanged a greeting.

"Morgen. Man, I am so glad to see you here. Your sister is kicking my ass at Liar's Dice. Can you please come and set her straight?"

He laughs. "Little Lin is beating you at Liar's Dice?"

The man glanced at Echo and me, his cheeks tinged-rose from embarrassment. "She did learn from the best…"

Throwing his hands up in defeat, Morgen takes a few steps toward the gambling tables. "You got me there. Let's win your lunch money back."

Wordlessly. Echo drags me as we follow behind the two men.

"Hey, Lin, are you stealing these poor, broke folks' money?" Morgen slips into a chair at a round table inside the dining room of the frat house.

Lin doesn't look up as she holds her glare on the man across from her. "Four sixes."

"Bullshit!" the man shouts.

She revealed her cup; two of the dice beneath it were sixes. Two were singles, which count as wilds in the game. The man had a single dice—a two.

He slams his chair back. With rage dancing in his eyes, he shakes his head, cursing, and leaves the room. The other players slid his losses down to Lin.

"You ready to have your ass kicked, Mo?"

Morgen's lip curled with a smirk. "You've gotten cocky since I last saw you."

Echo shifted on her feet, watching Morgen with narrowed eyes. The players shook their cups and Echo bit her nails with anticipation.

She liked this guy—really—liked this guy. And that infuriated me.

Digging my nails into my hand, I lean to whisper in Echo's ear. "I'm going to get a drink since you never brought me one."

She doesn't stop concentrating on the game, but nods and waves a hand. I take it as a sign and slip from her side into the kitchen where the game and music are less mind-rattling.

Except it wasn't quiet or empty.

The preppy kids of the College of Power encircled a few War College students I recognized from registration. They were hanging from their feet, drinking from a keg, while others shouted chants. By the time one kid finished, the other was throwing up. Chanting turned to boos and the booze fell from his lips spilling onto the floor.

Without a doubt, the College of War kid won the contest. We were known for having a strong constitution, but the College of Power kids could not help but pick a fight with us when they could.

The other colleges were more dormant.

The College of Evil kids were a cult, their identities secret. Paladins of the College of Fear were back in the living room corners listening to music with women and partners dancing in their laps, while the Strategy students were around the Liar's Dice table.

I would've been surprised if anyone there had survived

the semester if they had all had to fight each other. The academically gifted kids didn't hang with the fraternities. I wouldn't have, either, if Echo wasn't persistent. All this party did was look at some of the competitions at the College of war. Most, if not all, of the College of War was there.

"Hey, you. Dragon—kin?"

My head snapped from the deep stare I held from the doorway. One of the orcs dressed in Power College attire was staring back. "Nala," I corrected.

"Nala, would you like to have a go? I am sure you cannot hold up to someone like me."

The crowd around us started chanting and pushing me from the doorframe to the center of the kitchen. Before I could protect myself, they were turning me upside down and placing a spicket in my mouth. The hot liquid burned along my esophagus, but I guzzled it as my ancestors and classmates shouted.

It wasn't until the barrel ran dry and they sat me on my feet that I felt the world spin my head at a good moment. A woman came to my side, raised my arm, and said something incoherent. Everyone else responded with a chant.

"Nala! Nala! Nala!"

CHAPTER 2
NO MAN'S FEET

"**G**reat job." There was a pat on my back and voices calling out congratulations before I could stumble out of the kitchen.

When I said I was going for that drink, I didn't mean a whole keg of commoners' ale.

Sloshing with each step, my stomach turned and twisted with waves of nausea that had me searching for the bathroom. The wall skidded past my searching hands as I used the furthest part of the room to wade past the party. Dancers and fiddlers hadn't dared to stop what they were doing despite the party and heavy drinking. The music swayed a crowd of rowdy college kids who would have to start the most gruesome challenges of their lives in three days. The only people thinking of the fact it was Friday were the College of War kids scoping who they would murder first.

I could see the scales of Echo's skin from between dancing bodies. On the other side of the room, Morgen had her on his lap at the Liar's dice table, betting and lying with a new round of Power College kids.

If it weren't for the foggy thoughts and the hazy perception, I would've been more angry about them. But I was lucky to focus on anything, let alone how I felt emotionally.

The bathroom was another fifteen steps away before I joined a line leading into the hallway. It wasn't likely that I could make it there before puking, but my stomach had settled and I decided to slump against the ugly, green wall.

They are a bunch of fraternity men with no style. Decorated in various mysterious splashed liquids, the green was more vile than the booze. It gave nothing to the room but the feeling that all these men would be single due to their ability to clean up after themselves.

The crowd cheered with the last strum of the upbeat song I was tuning out with my thoughts. Someone elevated across the room and leaned into a mic. Her hair was a stunningly dead blue, and as her eyes surfed the crowd, she sighed the sound of an angel taking its first breath.

"Hello, beauties. I know we are celebrating being back at the world's top paladin school, but this next song is something I have been writing behind the scenes. I can't wait to finally share it with you." She took a breath and closed her eyes.

Captivated, I slid into the floor like when we arrived. I tried to seek out her features above heads, but she blended in from my position. So instead, I closed my eyes and listened.

When I'm taken from the deep,
I will not bow at no man's feet.
My mother and my father they taught me well,
With manners, nothing kinder than a backwoods gal.
A backwoods gal.

A backwoods gal.
I can be kinder like a backwoods gal.

But when I'm taken from the cold—
N' thrown to the dark and the deep—
I will not bow at no. man's. feet—

WITH A HYMN IN HER THROAT, A SOFT FIDDLE ACCOMPANIED HER, burning a harmony between her voice and the silence in the room. Tapping against the wood, her foot thudded, and together, the room clapped.

I will not bow at no man's feet.
at no man's feet.
at no man's feet.
I will not bow at no man's feet—

And when they prey—
My mama will'na stay—
She'll tell me to run, and I'll obey,
but I will not bow at
no. man's. feet—

I was'sa backwards gal,
withoutta' crown,
but a backwoods gal,
would've flown from town.

And when my mama could'a stayed—
I should've flown right away—

But a backwoods gal,
I'm a backwards gal,
and I will'na bow at
your damn greed.

"NALA." ECHO SIGHED. SHE SHOVED PAST A FEW CHEERING MEN to grab me from the floor. "Are you alright?"

I blinked at her and then at the bard disappearing from the crowd. The power of her song still resonated in my chest. My heart thudded too loud to let me think.

Echo's bows curled and I gave her an indescribable look before she took a sharp breath. "Let's get out of here. I think we've all had enough socialization for the night."

With a crack, someone's fist shot teeth across the floor. They rattled against the wood and all eyes turned to watch them settle as blood pooled around them.

"You bitch."

The woman spits, wiping her lip with the back of one hand. She winds the other into a fist that shoots across the shoulders of someone holding her back. It didn't take long for someone to yell, "*Bar fight!*"

Bodies slammed against bodies, hair ripped from heads, but Echo steadied me the best she could. We dodged most attacks together, but it was over once someone's fist smacked the back of my head. Echo's eyes widened and I cracked my neck, pulling from her grasp.

"Nala. Nala, this isn't a good idea. We should just—"

Before she could get the next word out, my curled fist crunched against the man's nose. His eyes rolled back with the rest of his body smacking into the floor. He was out. And a great nap that was going to be.

TAPPING MY FOOT, THE HALL ECHOED THE SOUND BACK WHILE I leaned forward in the chair. The school was quiet this Saturday morning, with everyone sleeping off their hangovers from the night before. I would've done the same if it hadn't been for the message I received from the Headmaster, bright and early. Sitting there for ten minutes, my patience was thinning. I was ready to bail, but then the door to his office slid open.

The half-dragon, half-humanoid man slipped out, his rounded glasses on the edge of his nose. With bags under his eyes, he was no doubt just as ready to end this meeting as I was.

We filtered inside and I sat in front of his desk. He rounded it before stopping promptly with both hands placed against his side. Dropping his head, he sighed. "Imagine my disappointment when I got a call at two in the morning that all of my best students were knocking each other's teeth out."

"If it's any consolation, the evening didn't start that way."

He shook his head and slipped into his chair. "Nala. We've known each other for quite a while. Your mother was my classmate at junior studies on Black Dragon Isle."

I knew where this conversation was going. I knew the disappointing tone that carried each word on his breath.

"You and your friend put yourself in a stupid position last night. This is not Mountainside Junior Paladin Academy. This is your last semester before your arena trial." His eyes narrow. "You will need to survive the semester first to take that trial."

I nod my head.

"Two," he said with a quick breath. "Two War College students died last night. Beaten to death. Witnesses cannot place the victor."

Catching my breath, my eyes widen.

"This is real life, Ms. Delvimir. You will be hunted. You will be preyed on by vicious lies. Do not fall victim—" His lip curls. "—rise."

I thought his eyes slid past mine for a moment, disappearing behind me. Then he rested back against his chair and crossed his arms. "What do you desire, Nala?"

"Desire?" I chuckled with a short breath, so quiet and sure he hadn't caught it. "I desire many things. But what I want from my education is different. The future I envision is one where I lead beneath my deity. Invoking his will and taking back everything that has been stolen from us. After all, that is why most of us are here."

I dropped my eyes to my hands, the scales neatly aligned until they wrapped around the deep scar in my palm. "We remember."

"Interesting answer."

But it wasn't the headmaster that spoke those words. A deep rumble rose from an ancient throat and took a step somewhere behind me. Lifting from the chair, I turned and saw divinity in its avatar form. Branded in his black and red metallic plate armor and standing only half draconic like Biron, Baalthor towered over me, his red eyes curious and calculating.

"Baalthor," I whispered. Without breaking the locked gaze, I lowered my upper body in a slight bow before him.

He only smirked in return. "Nala Delvimir."

"You know my name?" I countered.

Here Baalthor stood before me, calling me by my name, and I could've melted at his feet. I pressed away all the energy and excitement bubbling beneath my scales. I watched him as he watched me. Because Baalthor, God of War, knew my name, and there had to be a reason.

"I know many things." His hand rose, running the back-side of a talon down my cheek. "I know the look in your eye isn't from excitement, but pride. You take pride in knowing you've garnered my attention. Maybe some curiosity, too. But you do not care because this is what you were waiting for all those nights of prayer. You were waiting for the callback."

"I was waiting for fate to tell me who I should answer to."

He scoffed. "Fate talks about knowing one, keeping all the glorious answers to himself. But Nala, you knew. You knew that even with your mother begging you not to go on this route to Paladinship, this is where you'd be. You've always known."

His eyes darkened. "But what you desire is not what you said to Biron."

I swallowed, searching for the answer he was waiting for.

"Nala, I know why you longed to be a paladin and chose to side with me in this war. Your mother and father, just like many of the chromatic dragons, were exiled from the mainland nearly twelve years ago. Your father was almost assassinated and you took a life."

"You took a life at seven years old," he said.

It was so casual for him to reminisce on my life, but that wound embedded in my scales ached at the memory. I was pinned beneath a soldier, someone from the town church.

He was shouting obscenities while his friends held my mother back. My father was nowhere to be found.

Our neighbor, a dragonkin that had just settled, lay dead with a short sword pierced through her chest. In my haste, I grabbed it by the blade, pulled it from her chest, and wielded it to defend myself.

He cleared his throat. "They purged the chromatics and exiled what was left to the Isle. The Black Dragon Isle. What should be a sanctuary for our kind turned into an overpopulated prison that many choose not to leave in fear of execution."

His arm rose into a fist, then relaxed to caress my cheek. "You desire justice. For your friends, family, and home. And that is why you chose this path to Paladinship. That fuel is what makes you Biron's favorite student."

"Why are you here, Baalthor?"

His eyes studied mine. "Biron is the Paladin of my church in Crossroads, as you know. Call it business. But—"

He paused, took a few steps back, and wrapped his arms behind him. "I will be asking something important of you, Nala. Since Biron spoke so highly of you, I wanted to put a face to your name. And now that I have, I am afraid I must leave the rest of my endeavors until next time, Nala."

Biron stands from his chair and bows at his waist. "It was a pleasure to see you, sir."

But I stood there watching the deity.

"Farewell."

And then, in the warp of red mist, he disappeared from Biron's office, leaving me back to the awkward and exhausting Saturday that had started this all.

I dropped my tone into a whisper. "You could've warned me."

"And what fun would that be?" Biron chuckled. "Call it punishment for almost killing yourself at a fraternity."

CHAPTER 3

BLACK DRAGON ISLE

Saturday afternoon, I packed a bag and slipped the ruby gem my mother gave me on my finger—a family heirloom and graduation gift from my father. The silver band tied a glowing red ruby to my scaled hand and gifted me a set of wings. Since dragonkin don't have wings like half-dragons, my father used this for travel in the military. They let him keep it in retirement, so he says. My mother and I believe he could've very well stolen it, though.

But he will never tell, and Baalthor has never come to collect it.

Sixty miles southeast of the Paladin school, right off the coast of Guthrien, Black Dragon Isle emerged from behind the clouds. It always felt nice to fly, like second nature to my ancestry throbbing in my veins. But dragonkin were more human than dragons. Our skins were made of scales, but we had no wings. Just an overgrown body built like an orc, but shaped like a dragon.

When I settled on the island, and the ruby stone stopped glowing, Baalthor's voice returned to me. The island wasn't home to us; it was *just a place to live and stay.*

Water sloshed against the coastal rocks before pulling back into the sea. I watched it dance, taking breaths when it did.

"Nala."

My pulse fluttered.

Walking up the rocky path from the city's outskirts, my father bolted straight for me. Wrapping my arms around his torso, he sighed. "My beautiful daughter. Biron said that you were on your way."

"That bastard is up everyone's ass, isn't he?" I asked, pulling to look into his eyes.

Narrowing them, he glared. "Language, missy. Be respectful to others and others will respect you. He is a good man watching over his top students."

His disappointed frown turned into a teeth-grinning smile, picking me up by the torso and spinning around. "My daughter is the best Paladin in all of the world."

"Dad," I groaned, throwing my head back and pulling from his arms. "I haven't even passed my final semester and the other top two are just as good."

Sitting me down, he nodded toward the city and we walked back home together. "Other top two? You mean Echo and someone else?"

Keeping my eyes on the path, I cleared my throat. "She's just as good as me, Dad."

"So she did end up getting a position in the War College." He clicked his tongue. "You better not let this stop you from finishing your studies. If you drop out for that girl—"

"I will not be doing anything like that. We both know the circumstances we are in."

My father waved to a couple of bystanders watching from their shops and looking our way. A smile danced along his face before he turned back to me with sincerity. "You know I do not like that girl. I can smell trouble from far away. I'm telling you she is nothing but bad news, Nala."

"Echo has been my best friend for ten years now. She will not betray me. She's more likely to drop out of Paladin-ship to save our lives."

I wanted to believe those words, but a part of me wondered if her relationship with Morgen pushed her further away from me.

We took the next bend, spending the time climbing the hill on the other side of the small town with hungered breaths. At the top, he stopped and looked at me, raising a hand to place against my cheek. "There are plenty of beau-tiful and incredible girls in the world, Nala. Do not let her destroy you while you are still so young."

Pulling from his grasp, I cleared my throat and turned to walk up the rock road leading to our hut. "Baalthor visited campus."

His footsteps halted again. "He did? What did he want?"

"I assume he came to speak with Biron, but somehow I got wrapped in the middle of the conversation. We discussed the future and he alluded to a task for him."

"Nala," he cried, moving to take my hand. "That is wonderful news. My Gods, your mother is going to be ecstatic."

The rounded wooden door creaked on its hinges and my beautiful mother, all five feet of her, stood under its frame. "I hope the trip wasn't too bumpy."

"Mama." I smiled, wrapping my arms around her gently and leaning my head against the top of hers.

Despite squeezing me just as hard, she sighed. "What troubles you, little wing? I know you did not fly back here after a day gone just because you missed us."

"I decided to spend the weekends at home. It gives us all the time we can have together before the end of the semester." I pulled back to look at her and tears puddled in her lids.

"Do not dare talk like that. You will not fail the arena trials, Nala Delvimir."

A couple of footsteps rounded the living room behind us. My younger brother smiled when he saw who stood at the door and I embraced him. "Alfie."

"Nala," he gasped. I squeezed him tight. "Can't. Breathe," he wheezed.

Letting him go, he stumbled back with dramatic effect, acting wounded from the encounter. "Geez. You've been gone for one day and they have made you stronger. You're practically a weapon now."

"When did you get home?" I asked him. I looked at Mom and Dad, narrowing my eyes before looking back at him. "No one told me you would be here."

My brother chuckled. "I came home for the weekend yesterday. I had no classes."

"How was your first week at Mountainside?" I smiled.

Crossing his arms, Alfie shrugged. "Honest to the Gods, I am calling it now. I will be sorted into the College of Strategy. The map reading classes are so easy and my favorite."

My mother's face dropped. She dropped her gaze, moving around us toward the kitchen to leave the conversation. I watched her back as she went.

I knew she was proud of us for ending up anywhere in the world, but it scared her more than anything. My parents knew I'd be in War College like my father, which rattled my mother. She begged and begged, even going as far as getting me a placement into the Clerical studies at church.

But there wasn't anything she could do when I flew off for my first day at Mountainside.

My brother turned back to me. "I do love the mountains. It's secluded and nice. Although we don't have shops, bakeries, or—"

His eyes move to my father before dropping his voice into a whisper. "—taverns."

"I heard that."

We both giggled at him.

"It is beautiful up there." A wave of sadness riddled his expression and I knew what depressed him.

But I slapped him on the back and smiled. "Let's go help mom with lunch, shall we?"

DIPPING MY HANDS BENEATH THE WATER, I GRABBED THE NEXT bowl and scrubbed. Mom dried my previous dish beside me, too quiet for her usual demeanor.

"What is it?"

"Nothing." She shuffles on the next dish, hoping I don't see the tear gleaming on her scales.

Passing her the next one, I grab a hold of her arms. "Where's my fierce mother and what have you done with her? You never let Alfie or I sit in the living room to eat. You never cook the deep-frozen bison and veggie stew unless it's a special occasion. And you always—*always*—talk to me. So what is it?"

Drying the last dish, she embraced me. "The Isle's church has communicated with the mainlands and they are speaking of horrible things. Our underground dragonkin says they hear whispers about bodies on the shore."

"Bodies? On the shore? That's only an hour's flight from the school."

"I'm not worried for you. Biron will make sure that you are safe, but Nala...Nala, the Church of Light talks about pushing the dragons off the Isle and into the southern continent. It's a three-day journey and most of us cannot fly. They'll eradicate us."

I stiffened, nose curling at the thought. "Why? Why would they do that?"

"They say we are hunting the mainlanders, killing them for sport."

My eyes widened.

I knew it wasn't true. Most of the ancient dragons among our kind were dormant in the mountains and the adult dragons had created a hoard on the Isle. The dragonkin cannot possibly be flying back and forth. It cannot be anyone from the island.

My mother watched my confusion and contemplation with sadness in her eyes. "I– I think we will ask the church to relocate us to the mountains. We will be close to Alfie and the ancients would never be disturbed out there, so it will be safe."

"What? You can't leave. They can't." I huffed. "They cannot do this to us again!"

"I know, little wing. I know. But we cannot retaliate. Leaving will spare a war. I would rather relocate than watch our kind be murdered by Romar's men again."

I balled my fist and let the tears burn in my eyes. "I will speak to Baalthor. We will not let this happen."

"Oh, Nala, sweet girl." She caressed my face with those desperate, pleading eyes. "All I ask of you is not to let them take away your beautiful heart."

"I promise."

It wasn't the easiest promise I could make, but a challenge would always intrigue me. Nothing could make me unlearn my father's strength and hardheaded will. And as for my mother, I was sure I had gotten at least a piece of her heart of gold. Together, they had been aiding our people for as long as I could remember. Some islanders are old enough to remember the days before this place when my mother would deliver babies at the church and heal wounded soldiers. They trusted my father, who sat on the city council, to fight for Dragonkind, even if it meant standing up to the nobles.

I'm a Delvimir, and we do not let anything ruin us. We thrive and rise, which is what I planned to do.

So, I promised a few things. I vowed to keep my heart and promised not to let this go unjustly. In the name of Baalthor, I would make the world our home.

CHAPTER 4

WILL I FAIL?

Bag, wallet, notebook?

Shrouded by the brisk chill, I shivered and searched, lifting my covers and opening every drawer in the room. My notebook for classes was gone and I had less than five minutes to sprint across campus and be in class. How could I have misplaced it when I used it on Wednesday?

I whipped my head back and forth, scanning the room a third and fourth time until the sparkle of the spiral stuck out from behind the trash can. I must have pushed it off my desk a couple of nights ago. Falling asleep at my desk had been a nightly routine at this point.

Plucking it from the corner, the pounding in my head rattled down my spine. Shaking it off and heading for the door, a knock rang and upon opening it brought me face to face with Echo.

"Poor timing. Very. Very. Poor timing," I said.

"Sorry. But I need to ask you something."

She sprinted with me, leaping the stairwell flights until

we reached the ground. The battlefields were on the outskirts of school property.

"Nala," she called.

I huffed, out of shape from my lack of energy and food. "You have two minutes before I have to be in class."

That didn't stop her from keeping up. "I was wondering if you want to go with me to the city this weekend to look for a Homecoming outfit?"

Homecoming, Homecoming, Homecoming. I had forgotten about Homecoming. Last weekend, I was going to ask my mother if her friend could sew up my tux.

Gods' damn it.

I shook my head. "The city? Why would we do that? Flying back to the Isle would be safer, especially with the murders in Crossroads."

She quieted and I slowed my pace to a stop; the fields and my other classmates a couple of yards away.

"I just," she hesitated, "I wanted to do what everyone else does. They go to the city with their friends and dress up for a day. You know? I've never been to Crossroads."

I kicked myself a couple of times for it, but I nodded in understanding and agreed to go. "Tomorrow, then?"

"Yes." She lit up; glancing back at the class, she smiled. "Good luck today."

It took her darting off and taking a few steps, but it returned to me.

Unit test.

It was on the syllabus and she reminded us on Wednesday. The unit test on disarming maneuvers would be a demonstration in front of our classmates, one-on-one with each other. And I didn't like any of them. They were out for blood while I was here to study and learn.

At the beginning of the semester, Echo and I were

disappointed to find we were separated on different schedules. But Headmaster Biron ordered it that way, no doubt, to keep us from becoming stupid and forfeiting our grades for our friendship.

But Homecoming.

How would I go to the city and shop with her, let alone ask her to be my date? Of all things, this was the worst-timed inconvenience she had sprung on me.

"Nala Delvimir, nice for you to join us."

With an awkward chuckle, my bag slid from my shoulder and I joined the group in the center of the field. "I apologize for my late start to the morning, Mrs. Godyni."

With a lack of tolerance, she continues. "Last semester, you were taught disarming techniques from weapon to weapon. You will take on an opponent today as we have studied and practiced. One will have the weapon, a dagger, and one will not. You fight until either someone is injured or the weapon has been disarmed. This is pass-fail."

A cold sweat gathered along the scales in my palm. I was a top student, yet everything felt wrong today.

Weapon-to-weapon disarming was an easy pass for me. My father's backyard sword lessons were enough to give me a leg to stand on in Junior Academy, but they came in handy in those final tests. But without a sword...

"Rosha and Casey. You will be our first group."

The half-elf, Casey, drew the short straw from Mrs. Godyni's hands. Then turned and showed it to Rosha. "Looks like I'm disarming."

Rosha's pale hands shook, taking the dagger in her left hand.

I called it there. Casey's spine stiffened, rolling his shoulders and then falling to relax. But Rosha, she couldn't rest. There was an advantage that Casey would use against her. He was taller and faster; his half-elven ancestry gave him an advantage over humans. And we all knew it.

"Whenever you are ready, you may begin."

Rosha pulled her hands up before her face, bending at the knees. A tremble still shook through her, but her eyes became her dagger as she narrowed into concentration.

Casey could see past the facade, a smirk pulling a dimple into his skin. "My, my, Rosha. I am sorry it had to end like this."

But she lunged first, taking him by surprise. She rounded a backhanded fist along the dull side of the blade, her other hand thrusting into his abdomen. Doubling at the waist, his grip faltered and he jerked back from her reach. But it was clear she wasn't going to let him recover. Predicting his step, she moved in sync, thrusting a palm up against the underside of his grip and the other to his nose. His head fell back and the dagger sliced across his chest.

Like that, the little human girl, no older than fifteen, injured the half-elf.

Casey clutched his chest and stood in disbelief, like many of our classmates, but our teacher looked like she knew this would be the outcome. "What a wonderful demonstration of the power of concentration and technique. Fine job, Rosha."

She dropped the dagger at her feet and the pair returned to a seat in the glass, taking opposite sides of the group.

Whatever it was that brought her to Zen did a phenomenal job. My nervousness burned after my sweaty palms dried up. Something moves beneath my skin–not alive, but crawling. It prickled at my scales and ran down my legs, keeping me from sitting still.

If Echo were here––

Echo.

I drew a breath through thinned lips, like drinking from a pipe. It wasn't just anything on my mind. It was Echo and her request.

"Nodish and Nala."

My heart stopped. I was not ready. Not in the slightest. I could not go out there feeling like this.

The orc stood, stretching his hands above his head. "Would you like to draw?"

It was a fair fight compared to the last. Nodish was the same size as me, but did not have nearly the same discipline.

Standing, I took up the space in front and stared at the two even-looking straws in my teacher's hands. All I had to do was select the long one. A teething smile joined my lifting hand, and I plucked the short straw from her grasp.

Its length caught up with me and I hiked a breath into my lungs, holding it there to calm the beating in my chest. All I had to do was disarm a dagger from an orc. I could do that with ease.

I returned it to her with a smile, shaking my head as I turned to Nodish. The dagger already gleamed from his tightened hand. With a confident step forward, I let every-thing on my mind cascade from my body into the dirt. There was no Homecoming, no Crossroads, no Echo, just the tense muscle in my shoulders stretching out from my limbs, loosening with every empty thought and returning breath.

May the wisps of war bless me in trial and protect me in vain. Our lord, king of Hellfire, will burn in my blood and become fuel in my veins.

Amen.

Nodish lunged, dagger turned downward in his palm. I

jumped back, avoiding his thrash, and hurdled a hand against his attacking arm. Striking with his other, I took the blow to my face and didn't flinch, pushing off the blade with my arms against his.

"The great Nala, you have a bounty on your shoulders, missy."

"A bounty?" I strained, breaking his form and stepping back to avoid the blade.

He chuckled, spinning it between his fingers and moving it into his left hand. "Yep. At least half the graduating class wants you dead before the semester's final arena challenge."

No surprise there.

Carelessness danced in his left hand as he used my backing to gauge my comfortability. He thought he already won. But I wasn't backing away from him. I was calculating and leading him into a false sense of victory. When he spun the blade again and let his eyes focus on the motion, I lunged, slamming my body into his. Our backs hit the glass and he rolled up over a couple of times before the point of the dagger came down. I used the force of my arm to hold it back, striking with my other chest, but he didn't budge.

It became a test of strength. His arm moved back toward his body, away from plunging the dagger into mine.

"M—Maybe you can take me out another time." I winked.

But my scales slid against his flesh and I attempted to curl from beneath him in his instability. Peeling from my place in the glass, I hadn't considered the space between us and the angle of his dagger. When it plunged beneath my scales, I withdrew it, took the opportunity to shove him back, and stood with the sword in hand.

Gasping with hunger for air, a smirk danced and I twirled the dagger in my palm. I had disarmed him.

"Nodish wins, injuring Nala in their struggle."

"But I disarmed him," I countered, dropping the weapon into the grass. My blood was still fresh on the blade.

She plucked it from the ground and wiped it off. "Yes, Ms. Delvimir, but you were supposed to do so uninjured. He struck first."

Nodish chuckled, putting himself right back where he had peeled from with our classmates. My shoulders dropped and the burning wound contorted my features.

"It seems you should see the infirmary. You are dismissed."

With a huff, I walked back toward campus.

The warm embrace of her golden light wrapped my shoulders in ribbons of gold. It seeped deep inside the stab and mended the flesh back together.

I was stupid for letting him stab me like that. Careless. All Homecoming had become was a distraction from my purpose here. Nothing should've prevented me from disarming him. But I didn't account for spacing when his arm slid down mine. The technique was sloppy and under-practiced.

The paladin's warm cloth bit at the fresh skin and she wiped the remaining blood. "I believe you are as good as new."

"Thank you. I'm fortunate it didn't serve anything

there; otherwise, you'd have sent me to the Crossroads church for a cleric. Right?"

Her eyes darted from mine. "That is protocol. However, the city isn't the safest at the moment."

"I've heard of the threats. Do you know if they have found anything on the killer?"

"The bodies wash up at night. Young and old. All mortal, human-like creatures who associate with the Church of Light. The leaders are so convinced that the Isle is responsible, that they are not looking elsewhere."

I shook my head, sliding from her stool and moving toward the door. "Stay safe, Noka."

"You, too, Ms. Nala."

Despite Noka's blue scales, she came from Black Dragon Isle, like most chromatic packs. I only ever got to meet her after I started Secondary Paladinship. It wasn't uncommon for the Isle to be populated by all colors of chromatics. The name wasn't in connection to residents, but a statement named after Baalthor, the black dragon God of War. There wasn't a dragon on the awkward slab of land that worshiped anyone else.

But Noka was familiar with my injuries within the first few weeks. Not knowing bounds was my downfall. She had told me repeatedly that I needed to slow down and calculate. But I rushed into every battle, sword first.

I walked from the infirmary to the lecture hall on the east campus. My next class wasn't supposed to start for another thirty minutes and there wasn't a chance I'd return to the embarrassment I had left in my previous class.

It was irrelevant to wonder how the other students did regarding skill set tests. It was one of the few classes that didn't require constant competition.

Walking the cobblestone path, the infirmary door

swung open, hitting the brick building and shoving its back closed. Shouts accompanied the hurried woman. As I turned, intrigued at the rush, a couple of my classmates from Battle Techniques struggled toward her, carrying a body coated in blood.

The four of them struggled, pulling the student inside and disappearing behind the door. A soft-paced click sang against the ground; our instructor was dragging her boots at a slow pace. Her shoulders were slumped forward; tears barreled in quiet lines down her cheeks. With that much sorrow, the student would likely not survive whatever had happened in her class.

But that was how it was. We were war students, not only because we were trained to accompany the front lines, but because we were to go to war with each other to rid the weak from our ranks. It wasn't kind, but required. If we were to win the war, sacrifice was necessary, even if it meant our lives.

Turning from her, I went to class in the lecture hall, cleansing the scene from my thoughts and preparing to get on with my day. But I had been early, sitting by an open sill window. The room was dark and empty. I propped my legs against my table and leaned into the stone wall, watching the infirmary in the distance. I could see only the roof, but I still watched as if my classmate would be there alive and well.

Gods bless their souls in the afterworlds. May their souls be weighed justly and their afterlife be lived in eternal peace.

Outside the room, the hall carried laughter and voices. A pack of students filtered through the door and took a seat. The instructor followed, flicking a spark from the edge of his finger. Every candle lining the room ignited with the silent command.

"Take a seat, students. I need you all to open your texts to *commanding codes*. We will be learning the next section today." He shuffled the satchel along his shoulder and slipped a hand into the leather bag. With disarray as always, the halfling man muttered curses, searching for what he was looking for.

ECHO AND I MET ON THE OTHER SIDE OF THE TRAINING FIELDS. The battle-horse stables were about a mile from the colleges. In their last semester, War College students were required to take a class focused on steed fighting and control. We both took the class as an extracurricular the previous year. Not only was it a bonus to be ahead of all the students, but that meant we knew the stable hand.

"Creed," I called, waving at the horned man brushing down a horse.

His shoulders shook from the startle. The brush slipped from his hand and clang to the ground. He placed it over his heart in its absence. "Gods' damn. Never do that again," he scolded.

Echo and I chuckled.

"This is Starlight. She was a donation we received over the summer."

Starlight bent to pluck grass from below her, her long black mane falling over her eyes.

Echo was in awe, taking calm steps to approach before running her chilled hand down the horse's back. "Oh my, gorgeous."

.   .   .

We mounted Starlight together, the reins fitting into my palms. Echo clung to my back with a soft grip. She had passed her training courses. *Passed.* She loved their beauty, but feared riding them. After all, why does a dragon need a horse?

But when you don't have wings, what else are you going to use to travel quickly and on short notice? Walking to Crossroads would take twice as long, not to mention we would risk falling into a bandit's trap on the other side of the Kelti Forest.

I smiled and saluted Creed, then pulled the reins back and gave them a quick jostle. The school flew away behind us. Her hooves thudded rapidly, bringing the chilled breeze against our scales. Only a few conditions were considered cold when you were at least some part human. And somehow, the school climate sat right inside the coldest portion of the coast year-round.

Nothing stopped us inside the forest.

Echo hummed a familiar battle tune beneath her slowed breaths, using it to distract herself. Thirty minutes later, on the other side of the forest, we stopped at the outskirts of Crossroads at the public stables.

"Rule number one. We do not go past the blacksmith's corner. By then, we are too close to the church and I do not want to get in a brawl with those goodie guys."

Echo agrees.

"Two. We do not stay until midnight. The nocturnal creatures of the forest do not like being disturbed and Starlight's feet make the loudest noises in the dead quiet."

Echo tied her inside the stable, nodding to the worker.

The dirt road carried us inside the quiet part of eastern

Crossroads, which was said to have the oldest collection of buildings and businesses. The bricks were crumbling and people were no longer building houses here, but the elders and most senior residents were the kindest souls.

Rose Fabric's sign dangled from the building, falling from the clay and stone. An open sign shone from the door window. As we approached, the elderly human lady met us at the door, pushing it out with a hand and welcoming us inside. "Come on, ladies. It is freezing."

Her lips pursed as the door shut. With her glasses sliding down her nose, she pushed them up and gave us a look over. "Well, I am not sure you guys can get very cold. Can you?"

"Yes, ma'am. We still get a bit of a chill on our scales."

"Well, the wind can't get you in here. Not until the roof caves in." She pointed to the hole, splintering wood protruding from the ceiling. Echo and I both moved back from beneath it.

Just in case.

CHAPTER 5
(NOT A) SEASONED MURDERER

"What can I get for you two beautiful ladies?"

Echo looked at me before clearing her throat. "We are looking for the finest dress for our school's Homecoming."

"Oh, what fun. I have plenty." The lady's hand shook as she lifted it, motioning toward the wall in the back of the store. Dresses hung from a bar in all colors, textures, sizes, and lengths. "We do not get many travelers here anymore. Too many people prefer the town square and pass through these parts. The only thing we are good at getting these days are dead bodies."

I choked. "That is the talk of the region. But are you saying the bodies have been showing up on this side of town, too? I was told they've been washing up on the coast."

"It's a ten minute walk from here to there. The bodies stay down that way, but we've had blood spilled here, random trash, and law enforcement banging on doors. It's scaring away what little customers we do have."

She waved a hand and took a weakened step. "You

ladies, take your time to find something; I will be right through that door inside my office."

With each step, she shifts weight off the left side of her body, using a hand braced on her back for support. It wasn't until I tasted blood on my tongue that I stopped biting the inside of my cheek. Echo watched and waited alongside me. The same worried and confused look overtook her features.

But it wasn't only the dead people that my heart hurt for. It was everyone else living in fear that someone was out there, ready to take their lives.

"Look at this," Echo called. I turned and she was pulling at silk and sequin skirts. "What do you think I'd look best in?"

"Anything and everything, darling." I bit my lip.
Especially me.
She paid no mind, waving me off with a playful eye roll.

She would have seen everything if she had looked at me for one moment with her eyes wide open.

She went about her shopping, piling dresses into her arms. There wasn't much of my wares, so I stuck my hands behind my back and strolled toward the plaque wall. It gleamed, gilded in awards and recognition. Cut excerpts from the town paper sat with each one. From fifty years ago until last year, the elder had won an award for best service, talent, kindness, community service, and more. As I reached the end of the wall, it folded down a hallway. Pins tacked more papers against the wood, but were not as gracious.

The pin fell loose with a slight tug and the paper fell into my hands. The paper was smeared in tear stains and ink, but it was clear the subject spoke of a murder. Three months ago, a young human girl washed up—mutilated.

In eternal memory of Ms. Carina Seidyr

It burned.

The heartbreak and tragedy of this loss burned. I hadn't known her; I had never even seen a day of her life. But the blonde lady in the picture smiled as if she'd won a great loot. And now she's dead.

Why?

Why was she dead?

Why, why, why—

"Nala?" Echo peeked into the hall, holding a silver sequined dress. "Oh, good. You found the changing rooms." Slipping past, she slid behind a labeled swinging door. I pinned the newspaper back where I found it.

"So, who's the lucky guy?" I called.

She shuffled with a chuckle. "You think I have time for that? I have six classes this year. The papers are drowning my floor."

"I just thought." I coughed behind closed lips, clearing my throat. "I thought you and Morgen were getting along well the other night."

"Morgen?" She laughed. "Morgen is just a friend. We do stuff like that."

"Stuff like flirting?"

"Flirting?"

Clenching my hand, I pull back everything on the tip of my tongue. "Yeah, flirting. He had his arm around your waist. You sat in his lap. That man is coming for you."

Her quick hand whips back the changing room door. Written disgust curled her lips. "You've got to be kidding me? Can no one have a friend that's a boy? He's my friend. Only my friend."

The candle burning beside us illuminated her figure and danced in the eyes of the sequins wrapping her body.

The sheer lace showed her black scales dipping down against her chest and then again down her arms. It accented every piece of her existence like a goddess inhabited her body and I had the pleasure of seeing it all firsthand.

"Dear Gods." The words just slipped from my thoughts.

She blinked, shutting away the anger I had ignited. Her mouth dropped open, startling her. Behind her rosy cheeks, my scattered, roaming gaze embarrassed her.

When I realized we were staring at each other, I cleared my throat and straightened. "Uh, you—you look incredible."

"I don't know." She sighed, turning to look at her waist in the mirror.

I took a step forward. "You're getting it, right? I mean, look at you. You're perfect."

Those eyes came back to me with a sparkle and a smile. "You mean it?"

"Absolutely. Get the dress and let's go. I can find something more in my style elsewhere."

The old lady met us behind her counter, typing something into a writing board. Her glasses slipped as she leaned forward, checking her accounts for the price of the dress. "Two hundred gold."

Echo didn't bat an eye as she opened her bag and counted the money on the counter.

I knew her family had a wealthy horde, but I could never see myself dropping that much on a dress.

The lady bagged and folded it. I leaned forward and tucked my claws into the palm of my hand, trying to catch the worry before it fell on my lips. "The article...on the wall—"

Her shaky hand stopped moving. "My granddaughter...

She was a healer. But one focused on animals and their health."

Handing the bag to Echo, she pulled a photo from behind the counter and gave it to me. "She cared for every living being in this world and the next. There wasn't a person or animal that didn't love her as much as her family did. Now, that light is gone, snuffed out by someone so cruel."

Placing a hand on hers, I held it momentarily and stared at the old woman. "Somewhere in the stars, she's caring for someone or something else. Her light was not dimmed or snuffled, only shone somewhere new. When our sun falls behind the horizon, the dark creeps along our sky and casts into our buildings; she is there—her light twinkles from the beyond. Let the stars be a sign that she's out there, taking care of the lives she gets to love from beyond."

A sob cracked from her throat, and the counter held her in its embrace. She didn't say much else, but I turned and embraced her softly when she held the door and let us pass. "You have a beautiful shop. Thank you for welcoming us."

"Always. You are always welcome here. Take care, sweet girls."

As the sun began to dip beyond the horizon, the sky flooded with pastels. The shadows crept and lurked. As we walked toward the bar, I made sure my own followed in sync with our steps. And when it didn't, the clip to my holster came open and my dagger was braced in my hand. I searched around us. The vibrant tavern was calling a few blocks away.

"What?" Echo gasped, searching with me. "Did you see something?"

When nothing happened, I tucked my weapon away and returned to her. "Let's get out of the street."

STUMBLING OUT THE SWINGING DOORS, TWO DRUNK DWARVES laughed and danced against each other. They paid no mind to us as we shuffled past and entered the way they came.

There was a soothing, soft tune sung from a lute, something I recognized from the party a month ago. Echo noticed her, too, staring with something like infatuation in her eyes. All the feelings fell from me. She had seen this stranger and suddenly I felt invisible.

With a clear path to the bar counter, I took a stool and Echo followed. "Do you plan to drop out? Or are we going to battle to death?" I asked.

The bartender raised his eyebrows, took a few steps away, and found something better to do.

"I figure I will probably battle you to the death." She tapped a finger against the scales on her face. "Is there a better way to die?" she asked.

I didn't respond, swallowing it all down. Her smile faded and she turned away from me. "I thought we weren't going to talk about it, Nala?"

"So we ignore it? We pretend one of us isn't going to die, when we stand in the middle of the school holding weapons at each other, then what?"

"One of us?" She laughed. "Nala, do not sit here and pretend that we are equals. I will never be able to match you."

"I know you can fight, you just choose not to."

She didn't respond.

"What do we do then, Echo?" I grabbed her hand. "How do we get out of this with each other and our futures?"

"I don't know," she snapped. "Nala, I can't—I can't talk about this right now. I want to drink and stay happy. Maybe we will get a pardon or an internship by Baalthor before we graduate and skip it all. That's the goal. To work for Baalthor? Then we go to him and get out of here."

I shook my head and a tugging sarcasm pulled at my lips.

The bartender slid two beers toward us. "You look like you need this. It's on the house as long as you don't kill each other or anyone else in my bar."

Echo and I rolled into laughter. He looked more worried with each moment we said nothing, but stayed hysterical. We didn't know why it was funny, but it was better than crying. So we laughed and laughed until the man walked away. Then we drank. We drank it all away.

Another woman joined our strange lady with the lute, strumming a lyre. They sang and danced for the crowd before them. The later it became, the more worried stares we collected on our backs. No one stood too close, sat beside us, or said anything to us aside from the bartender. We became an infection to the people's night, but not one moment would affect how Echo and I balked, laughed, and talked.

"Who? Who is it, Nala? I know there is someone you are falling on—for. Something. I know something. Now tell me it all." The words fell from her drunken lips.

I laughed. "Well, I cannot. I have no chance if they have to die, anyway."

Eyes slid to me and a couple moved toward the door.

But Echo's eyes widened. "*A war college student?* Oh, my Gods, Nala."

She breathed. "Nala, that is such a bad idea. You have to know better–in our class? You are more likely to be killed by your lover."

"Y'all are drunk." The man behind the counter returned, holding out an empty hand. "Pay up and head home. I don't have the room for the trouble of drunken guests."

We were drunk, but not any more than anyone else.

People were knocking over chairs, spilling drinks, and singing too loudly, but we paid up and left regardless. Stumbling out the side door, we folded into the shadowed ally.

"Imagine if I found someone…" She began, tumbling into laughter between the words. "Someone I liked."

"That might be nice," I slurred.

She grabbed my arm as the door slammed shut. The night folded in on the two of us and I couldn't help it. Even in the narrow light of the half-moon peeping from above the buildings, she was everything.

I snaked a hand behind her neck, curling my fingers against her horns and pulling her to me. Her lips crashed into mine with a soft tug, tasting of strawberries and beer. There in that alleyway, her tongue danced with mine for only a moment.

My eyelids folded back and a shadow moved somewhere to my left. Echo pushed me back and I turned toward a scream where the edge of the buildings sat.

There was a figure folded onto the ground at the end and another who disappeared beyond the buildings.

"What–" Echo reached for my arm with her mouth

parted, but I was already heading that way. She snapped back into the moment and followed behind me.

The girl choked on blood and Echo dove into her knees to take her side, screaming for anyone to come save her. The wound gushed and a light faded from Echo's eyes as she begged the girl to stay awake.

It was too late. We both knew it. Looking at the wound where the blade had cut, splitting the skin wider where they struck, there was no question. Only a cleric could save her and neither of us was anything close.

Echo whimpered. "Someone, please."

"Echo," I whispered, her name catching in my throat.

"Nala," she cried. "Nala, do something!"

When I didn't move, her eyebrows knitted and she screamed. "Help her!"

"Echo, she's dead."

It wasn't Echo's first time seeing a dead body. But she still wept at the poor girl's side, not caring who she was or what her business here might've been. She wept for the girl she would never become.

This girl was supposed to kill her classmates and survive finals? She had too much of a heart, it would be her downfall. Her sword technique could be immaculate, but that does not mean she could kill.

I couldn't fathom Echo killing someone, let alone becoming a master of war and surviving beneath Baalthor. But yet she followed me here under the vice of her parents as long as she served in Baalthor's church. They would be set for life. The benefits they would receive from her service in the war would be plenty for them to keep their home on the island. She could not deny her parents when they asked her to do this.

No one believed she would pass Junior Paladin Academy, but she did. And now she would die.

"Echo."

Boots rang against the dirt ground and met my eyes fifteen feet away.

"Hey," a voice shouted. "Stay where you are."

Echo's hands shook as she lifted them from the body. "She's dead."

"We witnessed this only briefly." I strode carefully toward Echo's side, bending to take her arm.

When the soldier closed in on us and his hand drew a weapon from his belt, I yanked her from the ground. "Run!"

The golden gleam of the embroidered sun on the soldier's cloak flashed as he bolted forward. But I didn't wait to see if they would catch us only to talk. Echo sniffled in her gasps, but stayed steady at my side.

"They cannot follow us past the tree line," I called. The cobblestone turned into dirt street as I pressed against my best friend's side, pushing her to turn left between a set of buildings. She stumbled, but went as the guards lost a couple more feet from our tail.

Once we returned to the small strip where the old lady's shop was, we took off straight for the stables on the edge of town. "Almost there."

They still shouted, now from twenty-five feet away. They made the final bend as we approached the stables to catch up with us. Echo yanked the barn door open and dove through the building, looking for our horse. The stable hand cursed and shouted. As I looked back at the little lady's shop watching for the guards, I dove into my bag and tossed him some coins for the trouble.

Starlight neighed, jerking and jolting at Echo's lazy grasp. I pulled the reins from her hands and hopped onto her back. Settling under my control, Echo followed behind me, swinging her leg and tightening her arms around my waist.

"Halt!"

Burning in my palm, the reins slung down and she took off into the night. The soldier approaching swung a dagger that thudded into Echo's back. Her grip loosened but stayed. Her breath caught in her lungs as she cried, but once those hooves passed the tree line, we rode for a long, quiet moment into the forest's shadows.

"Echo," I gasped. "Echo, are you alright?"

She didn't reply, as if holding on and breathing were the only things she could do.

I pulled to a stop and swung behind me to grasp her shoulders. Sweat beaded on her brow, her eyes rolling back and forth. A soft cry came from the part in her lips, but she still held on and didn't loosen her grip.

A fire burned at my scales and I blinked it away. She would not die here. I would not let it happen yet.

"Hold on, Echo."

Hold on.

CHAPTER 6

IN LOVE &

When the headmaster scowled, a large crease ran between his eyes on his scales. Tapping his finger on his desk, he said nothing. I couldn't tell if it was me he was angry at.

"I know that leaving campus is not recommended. I apologize for the problems Echo and I have caused because of this."

His head snapped up. "You caused nothing. It is ridiculous that a couple of students cannot simply enjoy the town without being accused of murder."

It hit me then. What if it was a student of the College of War killing and maiming townsfolk in the night? After all, we are training and killing each other here despite the rules and laws outlined in our society.

"Have there been any updates on the murder investigation? Have you heard anything about the girl?" I swallowed, remembering Echo lying across her body.

He shook his head. "The only update is that a couple of dragonkin were lurking over a body in an alleyway Plenty of witnesses from the tavern can place you there."

"So they are blaming us?"

"They already were, but now they have *proof.*"

His hand twitched at the idea. Something was lost behind the look he gave the wall behind me. If the island were to be eradicated, his family would have to move away and the school would be without a headmaster—all because the Church of Light could not simply catch a serial killer.

Headmaster Biron has been at this school for fifty-six years. He became an icon after losing his leg in the war and retiring to join the church. Although this wasn't the only school for Baalthor's paladins, it had the highest success rate in the world.

"You and the rest of the school will need to stay on this side of the forest until the investigation on these murders are over. I cannot have any more of you getting accused, or worse, dying at the hands of the killer."

There might've been no rules about killing our War College classmates because of the nature of our studies, but Biron cared for all of his students and he took each loss personally. I once overheard him talking to my mother about his inability to sleep. This was when I was young and before I knew of things.

He said that he would stay up, remembering the faces of his students. My mother's clerical remedies only helped so much. I don't know what changed, but he had been headmaster for two hundred years at this point.

Maybe he realized this was how it had to be. We were going to be soldiers of war, bodies fighting celestial bodies and otherworldly beings. We needed to prove our toughness. So, Paladins fight to win a spot there.

I nodded to him, lowering my head in a slight bow. "I understand."

"Nala," he started, pulling my gaze to his. "This is not your fault. Do not let those town guards get to you. Baalthor will fix this."

Nodding again, I smiled slightly and stood up from the chair. He put on his glasses and began working on a previous paper without saying anything further.

The hallways were quiet at this hour. Due to the severity of the situation, the morning troop training had been canceled, and everyone decided it was best to sleep in a little longer today. Crunching beneath my boots, I walked across the gravel and peered inside the dark hall of the infirmary. Echo should be awake by now, knowing the healers and their abilities.

A couple of voices laughed and I pulled back the curtain to Echo's section of the room. Morgen stood over her, holding a bundle of daisies in his hand. The smile that was lit on her face told me everything I needed to know.

"Nala." Morgen sat the flowers on the table and hugged me awkwardly. "I cannot believe the two of you almost died yesterday."

Clearing my throat, I backed up and returned an insincere smile. "Thanks."

He returned to her side like a good dog. Maybe that was what he had become—her pet. Or was it the opposite? Was she his? I didn't know and that infuriated me.

I wanted to flee. "Echo, can we—"

Morgen clears his throat. "Oh, shoot. Echo? Did you get to look over those notes I gave you?"

A gleam in Echo's eyes faded and she turned to look at him, shaking off her thoughts. "Shit. I knew I was forgetting something. I can do it later this afternoon. Once I am discharged, I will curl up in bed and stay there for a few days."

My hand bled at my side as my nails dug into the palm of my hand. "Echo."

"I know, don't worry about it." She shook her head.

My mouth went dry. "You know?"

"You of all people know that I do stupid things when I am drunk. I get it."

The regret clutched me. "I–"

She looked up at me and there wasn't any attention behind the look. Whether it was the unspoken action between us or the wound on her back; she wasn't listening.

"—I'll talk to you later," I said and left.

The curtain fell back behind me and two voices danced again, no one calling after me as I left. Stomach curling, I worried and walked away, taking time to head back to my dormitory.

Thinking.

About her. About him. About what might happen now.

It burned. Angry from where the clouds snatched them up, the rain poured down and it burned against my scales. I quickly hurried into the building ten minutes before my history class began. The room was already waiting and most of the class chose to show up early. Whether it was because the weather or the interaction with friends, who knew?

Next to the paned window, I sank into my seat against the stonewall in the back of the room. It had been almost a week since I spoke with Echo and I was sure she was avoiding me.

I was stupid for kissing her, but I was even more stupid

for thinking that she would see me and listen to what I am trying to tell her.

"Hey, Zee."

One of the halfling boys from the frat group of War students stood before a half-elven girl's desk. Zee peered from behind her book, eyes dazed by the boy. "Yes, Luke?"

"Oh," he started, his hands shaking. He shoved them into his back pockets and averted his gaze. "Will you want to go to Homecoming with me?"

"Homecoming?" she repeated.

His throat bobbed. "Y—Yeah."

Her eyes widened, turning to pin-points. Then, as if a flood had come down against a wall, she broke from the stare and jumped from her chair into his arms. "Yes! Absolutely, yes."

I rolled my eyes, turning to the window.

Homecoming.

Why was I so hellbent on taking Echo to Homecoming, anyway?

My scales had been stuck, creased in anger and fury. Then it hit me. My scales relaxed and I felt the weight of it all come down on me.

I loved Echo. That wasn't a question.

But after all these years of inseparable best friends, she was choosing someone else, instead. And that hurt me. I didn't like Morgen. He reeked of lies and sneak suspicions. And if this were to be our last semester and memories ever, I wanted it to be with Echo—

"Nala Delvimir?"

Snapping from whatever world I drifted into, I looked at Professor Rolt. He was holding a book open to some page I hadn't heard. The entire room stared back at me. Swallowing, I straightened in my chair. "Yes?"

"Can you read from the page?"

"Page?"

"Page eighty-two. We are continuing in chapter five. Seeing as though you have an exam on the fifth Dragon War at the end of this week, it would be best if you listened."

I nodded my head and pulled the book from my bag. Turning to the page, everyone continued to watch, waiting, wondering.

Nala, the great *failure.*

Clearing my throat, I began.

WITH EACH STEP, MY HEART POUNDED.

Just talk to her about the kiss.

But it wasn't just talking, but determining whether we would be enemies or lovers for the rest of the semester.

The building door slammed shut behind me and I ascended the stairwell, taking my time with each step and counting them as I went.

I could ignore her—forget about Homecoming.

When I reached her floor, the small window peering into the hall shone empty. The stone was missed and weeds were growing from its age. The wood was warped and rotting.

Ancient history. This was about to be ancient history.

I hadn't noticed my feet moving and the confidence in my chest. Something about the weeds running toward her room brought me along with them. She was probably resting, her wound almost closed. If anything, I would bother her with this nonsense to find out she was worried, too.

If either of us was to be angry with the other, it was me. And I was far from angry.

The wood rattled beneath my fist and a soft knock prompted the door to open. Shuffling came from the other side, and when the door opened to her beautiful face, I exhaled the breath I was holding and smiled. "Echo."

"Nala." She smiled back.

I practiced the words in the bathing suite this morning, reviewing the script in front of the mirror. There was no one in the stalls and I prayed that no one would walk in on me talking to myself.

You are my best friend. I love you more than life. Will you go to Homecoming with me?

But I opened and closed my mouth, holding our smiles in my silence.

She pulled her hand to her hip and drew that smile into a smirk, raising a brow. As her lips parted, so did the door, and Morgen poked his head around it with eyes narrowed on me. "Nala? What's going on?"

The bareness of his neck trailing behind the wood seized my thoughts.

My open mouth shut, my shoulder dropping with a disappointed breath. I thought she would call my name as I left, but all I felt was the burn of her eyes on my back. Once the door to the stairs separated us again, I trailed the vines with my eyes. They intertwined like veins, running toward and away from the heart of the building.

And maybe they weren't leading me right to her.

Maybe...

Maybe they were leading me away.

The descent wasn't heavy or loud. After these few days, my thoughts had fallen quiet and something settled inside me.

She liked Morgen and that was okay. I wish she had given me the time to talk to her.

It was cold again.

The fae called for an early spring a couple of weeks ago, yet we haven't seen it. A brisk wisp of a chill brushed my scales and I shuttered beneath its touch.

Once my feet hit the sidewalk, they didn't stop. It carried me further and further away from the dorms and past the battlefield. It might've been cold, but the walk was lovely. Skies of blue peered down and showered me in a quiet calm.

The edge of the forest breathed warmth from beneath its branches, unusual for the way nature lies. Its green was burnt with brown and still dead in specific clusters, but there in its life was the calling of spring. There would be a day when no one noticed how quickly the green bloomed. It would be a marvel to stare at for a moment, to forget about the wonders of time again.

And I did. I stared at those branches, tracing the tree patterns with my eyes. If I wanted anything, it was my dad's fried squirrel on a late summer night. But we hadn't done that for years.

A breeze did not blow, but the branches moved. I noted it in my peripherals, not shifting from my seemingly unknowing stare. Whatever halted in the shadowed woods was waiting now.

"Nala Delvimir." His voice crept against my spine, provoking me in ways I couldn't explain.

It rose bumps along the skin and brought me to my knee, bowing. "Sir—Lord Baalthor."

Beneath an airy breath, he chuckled, snaking his complete dragon form from the trees and standing at full length before me. A fang stuck out from his smirk and he took pleasure in my nervousness. "Do you think you are worthy of my presence right now?"

"No, sir. Never."

His scales creased as he raised a brow. "Interesting answer. Most people say something along the lines of, *it's a pleasure to be in your grace.*

I shook my head. "It will always be a pleasure to be in your presence and before, my lord."

"Humble. I hate humbleness."

"It's not humility, but honesty."

He snapped forward, eyes narrowed. "Then prove yourself to me."

I blinked. "Of course. I have no doubts about going into the gauntlet."

"No." His voice deepens, something sinister lurking between his words. "I have other plans."

Rising from the ground, I pushed away every bump and worry. My spine straightened and with confident eyes, I lifted my chin. "Your wish is my command, sir."

"The mortals. The crossroad mortals are fools—foolish wretches who are threatening my land, my churches, my people. I cannot swoop down and smite them with a breath. It would provoke more than a fair share of death and war. I frankly want this settled quickly and quietly. You will take your top classmates down to my church in Crossunder and they will aid you."

"Aid us?"

"They will give you whatever you need to hunt and kill the serial killer who is ruining my reputation. I will not stand any longer for these mortals to blame pointless killings on Black Dragon Isle. And neither will you. Do you understand?"

"Yes, sir." I bowed my head slightly.

"Do this, and I will guarantee you a place in my Church of War. You will wear my symbol, harness my power, and uphold my will."

The ground could've opened up and swallowed me whole.

An out.

"Yes, sir. Absolutely. When do we leave?"

"Biron will pursue you with details." He turned and returned to the shadows of the overcast trees, disappearing between their sway.

I turned, not waiting a moment longer to dart back to the school.

A WARM FRONT CARRIED MOISTURE INTO OUR BUILDINGS, AND AS I pressed against the wood, the hinges on the door cried. Biron was sitting behind his desk, chattering-nothings coming from his mouth.

"Oh, Nala!" He stood.

Morgen and Echo turned their necks to smile at me from the seats before his desk. My heart hammered, but my knuckles thought about it. They were curling into position until the tight fist was too wound to be released on any man. I wanted to cave his face in. But all it would do was destroy her and I couldn't do that.

"Now that you are here, let's begin."

I took a stance behind them, not taking even a second to smile or look back. I straightened at his words and waited.

I will be waiting until *he* proves his worthiness to me.

"Baalthor has requested that I send the top-scoring students to the academy to deal with our issue in town. The church cannot be directly involved; otherwise, it might provoke the Church of Light. The Crossroads and Crossunder population would suffer if they were brought into battle."

His eyes darted to the wood of his desk, tracing its pattern momentarily in silence. It could be a prayer.

"You two have been identified as suspects, so you must act carefully. They will have no mercy."

"Neither will we." Morgen chuckles.

Rolling my eyes, a scoff draws his attention to me.

"What?" He sets his jaw, crossing his arms.

I laughed, shaking my head in disbelief. "We are not going to fight the town guard."

Morgen stands. "Yes, we are. They will hunt us and we can't just sit back and let them, Nala. Sometimes you have to put down the goody two shoes and man up."

Taking a step forward, the blue in my eyes startled him. "You are no man. So don't you try and speak on the subject."

"Ha—" He stepped away from his chair, meeting me eye to eye. "Do you want to make a bet?"

"I don't make bets with wimps."

Echo moved. "Nala."

But Morgen moved faster, his fit curled and launching. He swung and missed as I returned the sentiment. My fist hit his chest and Biron rose.

He flicked a hand and a spark ignited between his fingers. Space burst between us and we stumbled away behind the chairs. My back met the door and Morgen met the edge of the headmaster's desk.

"Let me be clear, Mr. Ritte and Ms. Delvimir, you are not to participate in killing each other until you are back on campus and the mission is completed. As of right now, if you even attempt to harm each other, you will be expelled. This mission will require teamwork—equally."

CHAPTER 7

QUIET

My bag tapped against my hip, swaying with each step downward. Biron was right; we needed to work together to search an entire city for the killer. If this were a task that a singular person could do, then Baalthor would've just asked me. Instead, he requested all of us—the top three.

Echo and Morgen were laughing and carrying on when I swung open the door and joined them outside the dormitory. That feeling dropped to my stomach again, that hopeless romantic want.

How do you love someone who doesn't love you back?

How do you let them go?

Slipping past Morgen's eyes, Echo's smile dropped and she nodded to me. "Cool. We can get going now."

Biron lent us two horses for the journey. Riding through the forest should take us no time. If we keep the same pace, we will shift north and ride around the city to meet at the point.

"So, Morgen," I began, "tell me about your family."

"Nala," Echo warned.

"No." Morgen laughed. "You cannot expect me to tell you anything when you are just as reserved."

Echo growls. "Why can't the two of you just get along?"

We looked at her with disdain that was clearly meant for the other. Somehow, we already knew our thoughts on the situation, but instead of arguing, I agreed.

"Okay, the Delvimir family is an alumnus of both paladin schools. My father directly served the Paladin church and assisted Baalthor in the war. My mother is a cleric now. After she graduated from Power College, she rejoined the church and learned about clerical duties. I am their successor. My oldest brother is a fighter and my youngest has just started junior paladin school."

"No wonder you're stuck up." He scoffed.

"I met Echo on Black-Dragon Isle when we were wyrmlings. It was best friends on sight. The trouble we caused our neighbors are still legendary stories the Isle kids tell each other."

Echo smiled, her eyes distant as if she could re-experience every moment again in thought. "It was such an amazing time."

"It was." My smile dropped. "And now we are going to be forced to leave again. So, if you don't mind, this mission is crucial to our home and future. Don't fuck up."

The blank look on his face bubbled my nerves. I didn't understand what had him in such deep thought. But he didn't say anything more, nodding and leaving it at that.

We all remained silent when the barn doors peeled open and a stable hand dragged along the reigns of two beautiful steeds, Starlight and an identical horse.

"You've met Starlight. This is Asphodel. He's a bit of a hit among the ladies."

With his mane drooping into his eyes, he bowed low in

a soft walk forward. His head came up, nudging it into my face. "Woah, there. Hello."

"The Headmaster commanded you to have the two best horses in our stables, but they are not war horses. Remember, they've never seen a day of combat, just training. If, for some reason, you get into it with the city, run. Just run. These babies are too precious." The stable hand felt the coat of Starlight before turning, nuzzling Asphodel. "Take care of my babies."

Morgen rolled his eyes and mounted Starlight. "Do you take us for amateurs, druid?"

"Not at all. But you are still students with stupid, little student brains. This is my livelihood you are borrowing."

I couldn't help but chuckle as I slid atop Asphodel. He shuffled uncomfortably beneath me before settling into place. "We will be alright," I reassured.

Looking between us for a moment, Echo deliberated who to ride with. She said nothing, taking Morgen's offered hand and sliding behind him on their steed. I also said nothing, pulling at the reins and beginning the journey.

The stable hand watched us leave, closed the barn doors, and disappeared.

"What an anal little man."

My jaw clenched as Morgen laughed. Neither Echo nor I said something in return and he took it with grief, his jaw angry. "If we run through, we can get to the other side quicker. It would take us half the time," he suggested.

"A thirty minute trot is too long for you?" I called back behind me.

He stuttered. "No, I just think if we are quicker, we can get this over with. After all, three days is absurd; we need all the time we can get."

Something worth anxiety rattled in his voice. I hadn't

heard the tone before, but it drew a smirk along my lips. I slowed Asphodel down to pull beside them. "Do you know what lives in the Kelti Forest, Morgen?"

"Of course."

Echo gave me a look to back off, knowing whatever it was I was implying would start yet another round of banter.

"The Kelti Forest has another nickname." I smiled as he waited. "The quiet forest. Why, you ask?"

I chuckled again. "Because the creatures that live inside the Kelti forest sleep during the day and at awake at night. When you ride throughout the day, you are supposed to do so quietly so as not to disturb the habitants."

The look on his face told me he was confused.

"Pixies, Morgen. Angry fucking pixies. Do you want to fight a clan of angry pixies?"

We were ten paces away from the edge of the forest and I pulled on the reins, coming to a stop. Following my lead, he did the same.

"Not particularly."

But still, there was that face.

His eyes were distant and his jaw was uneased. It was as if something was there, waiting to break free, but couldn't. And in a long breath, he nodded his head and gave up. "Fine. Slow and steady."

"And quiet," I reminded him with a smirk.

He rolled his eyes and began to descend into the shadowed land beneath the trees. I followed behind him. Echo whispered into his ear, but he didn't reply.

Swaying, the trees sang a rattling tune, a crescendo of noise. The forest was left in silence when the wind passed through. Nothing else dared speak. Birds didn't squeak. Nothing moved.

Just the trees in that sway.

The soft thud of hooves echoed in the quiet as we dared defy it. Their heads held up a little higher, eyes wide and watching. Even Asphodel knew what was here, asleep and waiting. His ears twitched, but he kept on. Starlight was the same. We didn't stop; logs, uprooted trees, and broken wood splayed across our path, but there was no time or patience to hesitate, taking our course the long way around.

With the sound of the sway in the rattling trees and the movement of the horse beneath me, my eyes grew heavy. I leaned forward a little heavier, my eyes falling harder on the ground.

The grass was worn on our path and moist dirt lined the woods. At first, I thought I was dreaming, but then, when I was startled by a bump, my head sprang up. The drips of blood along the path became apparent reality. The reins tightened in my hand and I stopped.

Asphodel neighed, drawing the attention of Echo and Morgen. Starlight stopped and turned to face us.

"What?" Morgen whispered.

But my eyes traced the dotted path and how it led away from us. South.

"Nala," Echo said softly, "what are you doing?"

"Blood."

The word was just beneath my breath. The trees stilled and the horses lifted their heads knowingly. Asphodel jerked beneath my control and I took a slow stride from the dirt path down to the bloody one. Cursing came from behind me before the hooves thumped.

It was hard to track the blood in the overgrown grass; we were lucky not to have encountered a snake. There was no chance I knew where I was going, but still, fifteen thumps later, a new noise joined the sways.

A gurgle.

A choke.

My back stiffened and I slid onto my feet, crouched and searching harder. Morgen and Echo dismounted Starlight. The look on the orcish man said he wanted to run. I heard him swallow every few moments, his body moving to the opposite side.

He didn't look. He didn't search.

Not even when the rattle of a gurgle came back did Echo and I dart for the sound. He lazily stayed paces behind.

But there she was—a girl. Her eyes were open, capturing the colors above her, searching between the trees for light. In her chest was the occasional impossible breath as she held on. Blood coated her body and her hands, but she clung to life.

Echo was at her first, looking for the wound and the source of the blood. It was all so fresh. Ripping her tunic at the end, she wound it around her torso tight and looked over a little more. I joined her, picking her up on one side while Echo gathered the other.

The girl's mouth parted open, a choke followed by a sound. "Giant..."

"It's going to be okay," Echo said. I wasn't sure who she was trying to reassure.

Morgen watched us swing her over my horse. He avoided looking at her as if this was all inconvenient and unimportant.

We all began to remount when a flutter caught our ears. The horses stiffened, and Morgen—Morgen's eyes widened larger than I'd ever seen.

"Go. Go. Go, now," he whispered.

But I was already turning the horse and leaping for the path when Echo screamed. The once quiet forest became unstill. Trees shook, birds came alive, and the flutters blended with the trees.

"Get off me!"

She threw her hands up, shoving away the bugs surrounding her.

Smacking the creatures that neared her scales, the beings surrounding her hissed and launched forward. They pierced her scales, their teeth sinking through them as she flailed around in their grasp. Morgen attempted to pluck them from her, but they turned their attention to him. More and more creatures began to show.

Asphodel startled from beneath me as I slid from his back. He shuffled a couple of feet back, neighing but remaining on the ground, carrying the woman. I drew my sword from its sheath. They might have been little pricks, but I was a good hit.

As they gathered, clumping and attacking in groups of four, I swung, knocking them from the air around me. The next one screamed, her body snapping and smacking into the ground. When she went still, the next bit with a more brutal force. I failed to pluck her, focusing on the others flying to get a good spot.

Morgen and Echo have slid from the horse and were following my suit, killing what they could. The first signal of a retreat excited me; fewer and fewer pixies were attacking, fluttering off somewhere else. When the forest quieted again, I sheathed my sword and ran for the horse. We weren't waiting any longer.

Raising the reins, they slapped down and Asphodel took off as the others fell behind our sprint. The ground flew past the hooves of the horses' feet, but that didn't stop us from feeling the shake.

The ground shook. Rhythmic, quick rumblings that

seemed to grow closer. Trees snapped behind us as a giant pulled them apart, roaring between them to catch up with us.

"A giant?!" Morgen yelled. "You said pixies, not a fucking giant!"

I whipped my head forward and released another scream at Asphodel. He launched harder through the forest. "To be fair, I didn't know about the giant!"

The branches seemed to curl around the exit as light shone through them.

Five hundred feet.

An angry hand the size of a small house swung down at Morgen and Echo. She screamed and the horse startled, pulling its front up. When she slammed back down, she spun and kicked. I pulled Asphodel to a stop, heart thudding somewhere behind my scales. Had it fallen to my stomach?

Echo clung against Morgen, but struggled enough to stay atop the horse. My foot slipped from the holster, pulling it against Asphodel's back. I stood, feet placed into his back, with one hand gripping his mane.

My thudding heart began to slow; another hand rose at a similar pace. Time warped beneath my gaze and I drew a breath with my blade. I was pressing my hand around the hilt and drawing my shoulder back.

"By the might of Baalthor," I whispered.

And it flew.

His hand. My sword. Our curses. Her scream.

It hissed beneath the trees; his hand had been on its way down when the blade pierced his left eye. He swung his body back and I climbed down. Morgen regained control of Starlight, and we sailed past the trees into the light.

The open field never felt more freeing. A roar brought retreating steps and the giant disappeared back to his home. But we didn't stop to consider it. The stables at the edge of town were a little further and we rode silently until we hit the gravel outside it.

"Nala!" Morgen called. "Where are you going? This leads to the city."

"We have to drop the girl off somewhere safe. The stable hand can call for the guard. He's not a quarter mile away from the edge of town."

We skid to a stop, hearts still worried about the giant and the girl. Her breathing had gotten worse. A man rounded the building, hearing us come up. There was a look in his eyes, something like hatred or disgust. But I pulled the lady down from my horse and brought her to him. "Call the guard and get her help."

"What in Romar's name happened?"

Her wound had reopened. Blood gathered in the cloth and I shook my head. "Make sure she has a chance."

He was still cursing when we took off again. The slow trot was nice once the building was no longer in view. The sun was setting in the distance as orange and red danced in the grassy plains. I watched the little sun peer from behind the distant city with hesitancy.

It watched back with malice.

CHAPTER 8
CROSSUNDER

There was a shack somewhere far from city eyes. No trees. No horses. No buildings. It was just a shack in the middle of nowhere—with eyes. Eyes of war.

The pale elves stood expecting our arrival, but with bows drawn. Welcoming, but not without caution.

"Nala Delvimir?"

I dismounted Asphodel. "Yes, Morgen and Echo as well."

They joined my side. Echo was quiet, shivering, and tired. Morgen seemed changed by the experience of the Kelti Forest, calm and focused.

A man dressed in full plate mail stepped between the elves. "Excuse the introduction; we aren't used to visitors. I understand you've come from quite a distance. Let us welcome you properly."

The group of soldiers parted and we stepped into the shack. Candles lit the wooden walls leading down into a cellar near the door. If I had thought it was a chilly night, the temperature dropped another ten degrees beneath the ground as we all shivered together. Each time we came to the end of one flight of stairs, we turned a corner and another set began. This continued for thirty minutes and at the final set, a warm glow illuminated as if the sun lay beyond the corner.

But it wasn't the sun.

It was a city.

An architect with the skill of the Gods had carved out an entire world beyond the surface. A city the size of the one above bloomed in the light of hundreds of warm artificial suns. The cavern noise boomed; music distantly calling, flutters, dancing, steps, swords clashing, conversation getting lost beyond the person they spoke with. This cavern was alive.

Echo's jaw dropped open.

The man who had led us down stopped. "This is Crossunder."

My eyes struggled to find something to focus on. "How?"

"Crossunder is a symbol of history, young paladins." He motioned us to follow him. There were still a few more sets of stairs before we met solid ground, but that didn't concern us. We watched the city under the lights as he spoke.

"Crossroads was the first city of the mortal realm—an overpopulated metropolis of opportunity and pleasure. Baalthor founded his first church a few thousand decades ago. Several Gods followed suit and the town had a variety of religions to choose from. That was before the war came to the Mortal Realm. When it did, it came to Crossroad's first. Beyond our knowledge, Romar was purging *evil* from the land. Baalthor retreated his people, losing to the numbers

Romar had compared to him. But that hadn't stopped his people from secretly retreating into the sewers and building cults. They built a tunnel system that turned into a trade route and Baalthor saw an opportunity. He carved into the earth with godly power and built this city with his bare hands. His churches and people secretly moved here. A new city of trade and fortune blossomed, unbeknownst to Romar's people."

"They don't know?"

He smirked. "I do not doubt that they know. Somewhere, somehow, these people know of our city. But what are they to do? Just look."

Miles of the city disappeared from us as we stepped onto the solid ground. A dirt path parting the town ahead was lined with bustling shops and shouting residents.

They were purged from the surface into a new place where they could be safe.

"Do you not worry that they will try to force you out?" Echo asked, repeating my thoughts.

He smirked. "No. Our numbers down here are double what they have up there. There isn't a thing they could do to us anymore that we aren't prepared for."

The silence was hopeful. We weren't sure if the dragons would ever have the numbers to fight back for their home, but we were sure we would try despite it. And this would serve as hope.

"I will show you down to the buy-and-trade district. That is where you can find new weapons and things to aid you on this mission. Enjoy the city while you can. Let's plan to meet at Lilith's Den around midnight. How does that sound?"

"Good with me." I nodded. "I lost my sword on the journey here."

"Well, you will have no problem finding a replacement. This is the city for it."

And he wasn't kidding. Rows upon rows of booths lined the streets everywhere. The smell of food curled in the air. It was fresh and sweet; you could taste it from blocks away. Pale elves of all kinds existed, their families even, as children ran in the streets—orcs, giants, minotaurs, centaurs; everything co-existed down here. Women danced along to music as a lute strummed into the sweetness of food. It was a fascinating dance. Not just because of the women, but how the city twisted and turned. It changed before my eyes into a quickened beat or a slower, smaller pace.

We turned down a street and the side shops turned into entire buildings with signs and lines along the path. "This is where to go for weapons. I'll leave you to it. Don't get lost. Lilith's Den is in the thief's district. Ask for assistance if needed, but do not offer money in exchange. You will be haggled."

"Well, I'm not sure what I expected, but it wasn't this," Morgen said. Something of surprise was written in his widened eyes. They searched the shops and wondered about something lost to me, but still, he seemed like a child experiencing something grand for the first time.

Echo didn't seem too excited, not like Morgen or me. She let the light dance in her eyes, turning and watching the world buzzing along us as if this was the Isle. And maybe that was what it was to her—another Isle, but to me, it was incredible. It was power beyond injustice.

I shook my head, eyes rolling at them both. "Come on, kids. We are in Baalthor's city. We are in the heart of the mortal world—a literal Crossroads. We can do anything, buy anything—"

A sign of gold and red beamed from above a wooden

shop. A glass pane out front of the store displayed axes, swords, and knives. "—and I need a weapon."

"Rose! Rose! I cannot find my monocle. How the hell am I supposed to read this!" a female voice shouted from beyond the door. As the bell rang from above us, I stepped in and she jumped from her place. "Hello, hello. Welcome to the Grand Retreat. What can I do for you, folks?"

The older human stepped into view and didn't flinch at us. Her wrinkled face folded into a dimpled smile and she welcomed us further into her store.

I smiled, lowering my head a moment. "I need a sword."

"Well," her hand unfolded, motioning to the left far wall, "I have plenty. Don't be afraid to browse. I'll be around if you need me."

Morgen lingered behind Echo and me as we stepped up to the wall. His hands were tucked into the pockets of his pants as he browsed the daggers, which were not far from us. With one eye on the wall and another on his back, I watched out for his nefarious behavior. A clicking sounded behind us and Echo screeched, not of fear or pain, but of excitement. A black-furred wolf with red narrowed eyes stepped out from between a couple of merchandise stands. Its front half stretched and he loosened a growl with a gaze fixed on Morgen.

Echo bent at her waist and clicked her tongue. I launched to grab her away in case he was not friendly, but the wolf curled in front of her, bending his head up with his butt displayed for scratches. She reached down and scratched right above his tail, and he kicked a foot; a happy, panting face replacing the cautious one.

Raising a brow, Morgen stepped away from the display and rolled his eyes. "A pet—wolf."

"Juda! Do not bother our guests!" The lady shouted from beyond the aisles, listening to our conversation.

"Oh, he is no bother, not at all." Echo's voice curled upwards into a pitchy awe and she scratched harder at the wolf.

I laughed. "I don't think he is for sale, Echo. And if he were, Biron would kill you for bringing him on campus."

Flipping the bird, she rolled her eyes and I returned to gaze at the selection of swords. Long swords and short swords—enchanted and fascinated—but none called to me. If I was going to blow a fortune on a weapon, it had to be the one.

I walked to the counter, leaning against it. "For your most basic blade, what do you charge?"

"Basic? As in sword?"

"Yes."

She blew a breath, looking up calculatingly. "I'd say a short sword is twenty gold."

"Twenty gold?" I laughed. But she was not laughing with me.

"Yes."

"And a longsword?"

She thought for a moment. "Fifteen."

"Fifteen," I repeated. It's a little more reasonable to my standards. I shuffled the belt along my waist, reaching into my pouch and retrieving pieces of gold. "Here."

Her hardened look turned to a smile and she tucked away behind the display case, pulling up a simple, long sword and placing it on the counter. "Fantastic doing business with you, ma'am."

We walked out of the store and glanced around at the other shops. "Do we even need anything else?" I asked.

Echo looked around. "Potions, maybe? But I don't see

why we couldn't just deal. There's three of us and one killer. We should be fine."

"Yeah, but if all else fails, I do have a little healing magic and at least one healing potion in my things."

Morgen fiddled inside his pocket, pulling a jeweled dagger and spinning it between his fingers. I noted it earlier, displayed on the shelf he stood next to while Echo was with the wolf.

"I thought you were training to be a Paladin?"

He raised a brow. "I am. What are you implying?"

"Well, thievery typically sticks to the rogues."

His brow settled and his lips curled into a smirk. "I know."

It bothered Echo. Her eyes were fixed on the blade as if it symbolized something concerning. With a swallow, her throat bobbed and I realized it was guilt and regret, not concern. While on duty, she had distracted the guard dog as he stole from the poor, hard-sighted lady.

I leaned toward her ear. "Don't you dare take his choices into your own hands—you are not responsible for his actions."

"I know," she snapped. I withdrew from her side, staring at her momentarily.

Morgen took off walking, whistling and spinning the dagger. "Come on, girls. The fighting district sounds like fun."

We followed the sound of shouts and lines of people filtering down the hill into a compact center. An arena had been thrown up and hundreds of eager and waiting guests curled around it. A woman with pointed ears, dressed in leather, and adorned in muscles like no other elven lady steps up to an orcish man. Her face was creased with intent and she held up two wrapped fists while waiting. When a bell rang, her feet shuffled forward, her fist crunching into the man's face. He hadn't expected her to throw the first punch.

Withdrawing a step, she followed. His gut curled around her right hand and his jaw shifted from her left. He swung and she ducked. He attempted to retreat and recover. There was air beneath her feet as she moved on their pads; everything she did was anticipated and counted. He tried an assault, catching onto her patterned movements, but she faked it, pulled back, and swung a right hook that took out some teeth. Falling backward into the railing of the arena, shouts and cheers exploded. Hands came through to hold him still. He wiggled and writhed in their grasp as she knocked him clean out with a final punch.

That bell rang and the cheers erupted again, harder this time. Coins were thrown as refs and new people lined up to take on his barbaric elf.

Morgen starred in disgust. "Women...in fighting sports?"

Echo and I looked at him, but I laughed. "I dare you to go down there and put her in her place."

"Nala," Echo groaned. "Don't start this again."

"Fighting is not a manly sport. You do not get to gatekeep it simply because fate determined men should have a heavier build. Look at her. She's strong," I argued.

"She's a barbarian elven lady; of course, she's strong." He rolled his eyes and walked off. "I'm not listening to this feminist bullshit."

Echo followed him and I slowly did, too, but both my eyes still watched the lady pummel the next man who had entered the ring and challenged her strength.

What a woman.

"Wait up, assholes," I called, running after them.

"Aidre—WINNER!"

Echo and Morgen were whispering to each other when I joined them. The fighting district was growing quieter.

"Do you know where you are going?" I asked.

Morgen plucked a map from his pocket.

I stared at it in his hands. "When did you get that?"

He only smirked.

Walking another couple of blocks, the stores turned to homes and buildings of businesses that were not like shops. They were adorned with banners and symbols of Baalthor's war church. People didn't walk this street like the others. Those that did pass by were quiet and cloaked.

"Are you sure we are going the right way?" Echo asked.

We were about to cross a four-way intersection when Morgen stopped, staring at the map. "It should be—" He twisted his neck to peer down the road to our left. A sign lit with a hanging lantern swung back and forth.

Lilith's Den

The little wooden shed of a two-story building vibrated —a voice of seduction calling in tunes of majestic sound. When Echo pushed open the door, it was empty, or at least unpopular. Two people sat at a bar, sipping beers out of wooden mugs. A few women were entertaining a singular man on the stage, where a seductive voice called into a mic. It wasn't until we were further inside that the hallway bent into rows of clothed booths. The man we expected to meet sat quietly with his partners.

He raised a hand, motioning us over into the quiet area.

"Nala, Echo, and Morgen." He introduced us to the new men with him. "These two are my closest comrades. They will also teach you about the plan and how to navigate the city by tunnel.

I nodded, hurrying into the booth. There wasn't any room for Morgen, but Echo joined me just fine.

"What *is* the plan?" I asked.

I could notice him better now that we were face to face under a dim light. His dirty brown hair clung to his forehead. Whether it was a natural choice of color or plain dirt was unclear. A deep trench carved and scarred into his pale, gray skin was embedded beneath the strands.

Dark elves were not common on the surface. He had been the first I'd seen, and although that may have been, it wasn't startling. His eyes were a pale white and his skin may have been gray, but otherwise, he was like any other elven man I'd encountered.

He straightened his back, raising an arm above his head with an eyebrow following the motion. "Are you listening?"

"Yes, sir."

He smirked in reply but shook it off. "The killer has only attacked in a trifecta of places nearing the border of Crossroads closest to the school. We believe he has been using cloaking magic or the same tunneling system we use. However, despite our efforts, we have yet to catch him."

"Him?" Morgen crossed his arms. "Is this an assumption? After all, if women can be in fighting sports, I think they could be killers, too."

I rolled my eyes at his sudden epiphany.

"No, one of our men caught his build outside a club early one morning. He was leaving a trail of blood. It wasn't his own, but a woman's, the same one the guards found later."

"Interesting."

Echo looked up at where he stood and gave him a look I

didn't catch from where I was sitting. Morgen said and did nothing in response.

"You will take Henry with you." He pointed to the man on his left. "He is the best tracker and knows the systems well. We will wait until dusk tomorrow to begin your first day of search. I know your late travel tonight cut your time by a day, but if I am being frank, you will not catch him even if you have a week."

"Is that a challenge?" I smirked. "Because I am great at challenges."

"No, just a realistic perspective. We have been tracking him for months. Wherever he comes from and goes to, it's not here. He vanishes after each kill."

"How?" Morgen presses, leaning forward.

Echo watches him.

The man shifts, his lips parting to release a breath. "We don't know that, either."

"What a good lot you are. What even is your job?"

"Morgen," I snarl. "You do not dare question them."

He doesn't press forward anymore, rolling his eyes and stepping back.

"Anyway, Ramon will be showing you to your rooms." The man on his right stands from the booth and motions with a hand. "We will all meet again tomorrow night in the same spot."

We parted ways following this man's lead. A small inn-like area was in the back, up the stairs of Lilith's Den. Each wooden board creaked as we ascended. It splayed into a hallway of thin boards with rows of labeled doors.

"Seven. Echo." He pointed with a wrinkled finger. She nodded, looked at me, and entered the labeled room.

"Five. Morgen."

Morgen disappeared into the room adjacent to her.

"Six. Nala."

I nodded in a soft bow to the man and he did the same, disappearing back the way we had come. Across the hall from the love birds, I twisted the nob and settled inside. My sword clanged onto the small desk and my pack fell beside it. A nice hay-loft bed called my name and I sunk into it just before my door rattled with a soft knock. One I knew well.

Echo twisted it open and peeked a head inside. "Can we talk?"

I motioned her heavy red eyes inside and she closed the door behind her, joining me on the bed.

CHAPTER 9

WOULD YOU MIND?

She pressed my blanket into her face and sighed. Every few moments, she would draw back a sniffle and breathe out a heavy sigh. I tried not to disturb her—whatever it was, she took a lot of thought to bring the idea to her lips. Whatever she hoped to share with me was heavy. I wanted to allow her to gain the strength to share it with me without any push.

Echo used to share everything with me until Morgen became a wedge this semester.

I sat back against the wooden wall on my side of the bed and traced the pattern of the cotton sheets above the hay. It wasn't a terrible little bed for a makeshift inn.

"I don't know how I feel anymore."

The words caught me off guard. I knew this was about him, but I didn't expect her to share. My hand continued to trace and I waited for her to continue.

"He is not who I thought he was." She looked up, eyes glistening with tears. "He made all these promises to me and I fell, Nala. I fell so hard for the trickery of it all and now —now I am so deep within his bullshit. I am scared."

I sat up. "Scared? Is he threatening you?"

Her head shook and she met my eyes. "No. Not like that."

When she broke eye contact, mine moved to the door as I imagined the orcish asshole across the hallway jacking off to his god complex.

She sniffled again and her voice cracked. "Today, in that store, he had the money to pay for that dagger and the map. He has plenty of money. But now I feel that he only did it for show. Why would he do it for the show?"

"Men are stupid."

The seriousness in my eyes made hers widen; if realization was evident, something was coming to light in her thoughts. We held there a moment longer and then sadness, fear, and anger broke from her features. Her scales creased into a smile, and eventually, she broke into a laugh. "Men *are* stupid."

Her body fell into my lap and she pulled the blanket over the both of us. Her cool touch warmed mine and we lay there long. A snore escaped her parting lips when I knew she was asleep; I leaned to her ear and whispered. "I love you and won't dare let him ruin you, even if you choose him."

Then I followed behind her, snoozing off into the early morning hours.

She was gone when my body alerted me in the midday hours. The sun did not pry into the sills of the window, but that underground unnatural light did. My eyes found the clock on a nearby wall. It was nearly noon, which meant I could sleep for another six hours without anyone disturbing me. However, I didn't. I sat up and withdrew from the blanket that still smelt like her. My things fell naturally around my waist; bag and sword. Then, I sought out brunch.

"Would you mind shutting the hole you speak out of and chewing the food you are spitting from your lips?" Echo snapped as I found her sitting beside Morgen at the bar. She had a plate of fried eggs and some pork.

"Okay, I will be having whatever that is." I smile, pointing at her plate.

She slid it over. "Here. I am not that hungry."

I gave her a look and she waved it off, following it with a smooth sip of whatever was in her glass. The pork glistened with churned butter spread across the creases in the meat and the eggs still rolled steam from them. Devouring both was an act of Gods and I took my time with each bite. "Heavenly."

Morgen and Echo both stared and it took a double-take to notice. "What? It is quite good for a small place underground. Plus, Biron's chefs are nothing compared to Isle food."

Echo laughed and that smile I had missed came around. She poked with a fork, took a bite of the small piece left on Morgen's plate, and eventually agreed with my comment, moaning around her fork.

THE CITY WASN'T AS LOVELY THE SECOND TIME THROUGH. THE dirt beneath us shuffled. It dusted around us as people packed into the streets. If I hadn't been dazzled by the magic of the pretty side of the city, I would've seen this the first time, too. Dogs rattled their cages, barking at people passing by. They weren't meant to be pets; I knew it too well. Coins were rattling in the hands of rich, gambling men, waiting for a chance to bet and plead in loss. There was more than that, too—wyrmlings, cats, bugs, and so much more waiting to be sold.

Smoke rose before a food cart, blocking the view down the alley. My head snapped towards a wailing. A man was screaming, bent out of shape on a table. Two people held him down as another shoved a needle dripping in black liquid into his human skin. Each time, the man would cry out for him to stop, but the others laughed, which shut him up. I couldn't tell if he was there of free will or by force.

"The scums have always been this way. Every city has them," the man said.

"Are you from here? Crossunder, I mean." I replied.

The man slowed to walk beside me, Echo and Morgen falling not far behind. "I'm a scumrat. Born and raised in the above city scum, but moved down here not so long after. The guy who brought you down here found me a few decades ago and gave me a home."

"In the church?"

He nodded. "These people are just survivors. The city is too clean for them. Generational wealth infected our city like the others, leaving us behind in economic growth. Many people cannot afford half the things the poorest city man can. So, the scum rats trade and bet, living off that."

"Does Baalthor know it's this bad?"

"Baalthor does not meddle with this part of the world. He has things outside the veil to worry about. Our city is not the only one suffering due to the war. Cities with most of Baalthor's following cannot grow crops because the sun scorches the plains. He has turned beautiful places into deserts. Then there is the financial crisis. With crops becoming harder to grow, the gold cost has risen. All the mining down here has dried up and we are running out of wealth. All while the above city collects it and donates to the Church of Light."

"I didn't know it was that bad."

"You're young and from the Isle. Baalthor's churches here prioritize importing food and products from the Isle. Don't get me wrong; I understand why, but we are struggling, too."

He fell quiet at the city's edge and motioned us into the mouth of a pipeline big enough for a giant. It tunneled into a vast nothing, a bare gray dusting over unknown shapes beyond us. As he joined us last, he clicked his tongue and illuminated a small ball of light between his fingers. Then, dropping into a whisper, he leaned in. "We have to go the long way up. Do not speak too loud. These tunnels carry noise for miles and the above use them, too. We don't want to alert them of our presence."

The three of us nodded.

The unknown substance surrounding our feet didn't feel so wrong with the light. It was easy to pretend it was just water. The smell burned my nose, but I was numb after half an hour of trudging through it. Echo looked like she was going to be sick. Her face had paled and I noticed how she would intermittently breathe to avoid the scent. She'd wrap an arm around her face, draw a long, slow breath, and then release it over another few minutes. Every time, she'd gag and grow a little more pale.

But Morgen didn't flinch. His face was that cool calm he wore so well; I could never tell if it was a facade or if he was just soulless.

The tunnel carried a noise two miles into the walk and

we froze. There was no indicator of where it came from since the sewers climbed and bent in hundreds of directions. Noise would come more often the higher we rose through the system. I was impressed the man could navigate so well, remembering the way. He hadn't glanced at a compass or a map the entire time. Two eyes forward into the darkness ahead, stomping quietly into the waste of the cities above and below.

When we finally stopped at a ladder two hours later, he gave us the go-ahead to climb up. On the other side of a drain lid was an alleyway we gathered into.

Morgen helped Echo out and onto the ground to sit and breathe a little better. Her eyes were not focusing well and she seemed a little lost.

It had been raining, so the ground was soaked. The sun had fallen away for the day. I was glad of it, too. But still, people shuffled in the distance ahead and the long ally narrowed further toward a bustling street.

"Our church travels through the city one of two ways. You can climb," he pointed toward the towering buildings around us, "or you can travel by sewer from place to place."

"Please," Echo slurred. "I cannot do that all night long. My head is spinning."

"That would be the lack of oxygen from improperly breathing the entire time we walked," he called her out.

She flinched. "Listen, the stench was horrific. I care for my health and my lungs. There is no chance I am going to breathe that in willingly."

He held up his hands. "I didn't say the journey would be pleasant."

"Rooftops it is." I cut off the conversation and moved to Echo's side. My hands were already warming with a golden pulse. Her scales tried to recoil, but the magic leapt and eased away the fatigue.

When her chest rose, her eyes fluttered shut. "Thank you."

The rope hung above us, lying against the stone building. I climbed first and the rest of the group followed. The city's systematic design expanded in front of my eyes, and in that cool, post-rain breeze, I stepped forward to take it in.

Crossroads wasn't just a name, but a title. Every road in the city led to the center and away to somewhere else. We had come up from the underground somewhere on the western side. But even so, every part of it was lit and filled with life. Even without the sun, the world still went on.

"We will need to make our way south. The killer has stayed closer to that side to access the coast."

I turned to him. "That is where the bodies are turning up. How is he getting them from the city to the beach?"

Morgen joined my side, Echo behind him. "Well, maybe he has magic. If he hasn't been caught, then he is good at hiding. Should we not consider that he is using magic to move around?" he suggested.

"We've caught tracks in the sewers and felt the aura of magic, too. Whatever he is doing, it's a combination of both," the man said.

Morgen seemed irritated at the man's response, saying nothing to dispute or agree.

"Are you ready?" The man turned to me. A smirk crawled across his scarred face and brought to life adrenaline in my body. His foot twisted, his body following behind it, and he leapt from the graveled roof, catching air between the impact of his feet each time. He lifted a leg over the edge in the sprint and pushed off from its stone.

My heart pounded, watching him land on the other side. He didn't stop there.

My body buzzed and I took off behind him in its stirring. When I reached the edge, I leaped. Every scale vibrated in weightlessness and burned when my feet hit the rooftop on the other side. Calling from my throat, I hollered joyfully and ran after him. Echo and Morgen didn't hesitate, that soldier part of us coming to life under the city sky. Echo laughed and the uptight, orcish man with her did the same. A genuine smile and laugh rattled in his chest, making him seem natural for the first time.

"You're slow," I called back to him.

He smirked and crossed the next roof a little faster, his impact on the other side a little more complicated. He didn't fumble for a moment. Echo stayed at his side, but still, they didn't catch up. We crossed the western city in twenty minutes and stopped in a quiet part.

The man pointed ahead at a taller building. "That tower has the city's best view in case you need a better perspective. Stay inside the trifecta of this part of town. This is where the most activity has happened. Meet me at the drain when you are down for the night."

We nodded and he departed, disappearing into the night.

Slipping down the building and back onto my feet, I ducked behind some crates and watched the street as the others followed. A man dressed in silver plate armor, chuckling to a friend, walked past the end of the alley. They paid no mind to what lurked in the shadows. When it was clear, we crossed the road before anyone could see. No one was shopping, bar-hopping, or even chatting around the cloudy night. This part of the city was dead.

It made sense when Echo pulled a poster from the stone building. "Look."

Words painted in cursive ink read about a curfew on this side of the city. Patrol times were listed from dusk until dawn.

"How is the killer avoiding the guards?"

No one had an answer.

The paper clung to a puddle as I let it slip from my hand. We snuck across a few more roads and down another ally before climbing the tall tower. A bronze bell was stationary at the top. We ducked around it to peer to the ground. The only people moving below were the Church of Light.

"Do you believe they are doing this?" Morgen slipped beside me, nodding down to the watchful guards.

I hesitated to shake my head, but did. "I couldn't imagine them doing such a thing. Why would they kill innocent people to frame the Isle? It's counterproductive."

"How so?" He glances back with a side eye somewhere behind me. I wondered if Echo had been giving him a look.

"Think about it. The Church of Light blames Baalthor's people; they have a reason to attack. They've hated the Isle for as long as it has been created. This would be a reason to exterminate the vermin living on it."

My lip curled into a snarl. "Watch who you call vermin."

"I only repeat what they say. It is not my opinion."

"What is your opinion then, Morgen?"

Shaking his head, he lowered a gaze into the network below, a hand dropping over the edge and his head leaning into his arm. "You are right about me, Nala."

I raised a brow.

He continued. "I was raised rich, adopted by a wealthy elven couple. My mother and father worshiped the ground I walked on and paraded me with gifts and anything I wanted. The elven kingdom we lived in knew them like royalty, even the king."

The crease in my brow relaxed, and as he opened up, that authentic part of him returned.

Hesitating on the words, he did not look away from the city. "My mother died first. Late one night, a massive dragon swept through our lands and killed many. The Church of Light would not aid us in rescuing our family and friends from the rubble. We sent for help, but they did not come. When it circled back, it killed most of the people remaining. My father and I slipped underground just before it."

"A dragon? Do you know what kind?"

He shook his head. "No. It was too dark. But everything burned."

My eyes widened—a red-scaled dragon. Their throats were designed to create and spew fire.

"My father brought us hundreds of miles across the world to here, Crossroads. Then he drank so much that one day he didn't come home. I've been making my way ever since."

I stared down at the city where his eyes were now. "Well, it is an honor to be your classmate. I am glad you are here."

Snorting, his body shook, cringing back from the words. "Oh, Nala. You do not have to lie with such grace."

"No, I mean it. You will be a worthy opponent; that's all I could ask for."

He said nothing about that and the rest of the night fell silent. The Church of Light watched the night from below and we did so from above in that clock tower. Just before the sun could break the horizon, the grays of the morning and birds' songs sang us back to that alleyway with the drain. Our guide was waiting there when we arrived.

"Catch anything good?"

"Nothing." I sighed, my eyes heavy. But the travel hurt every scale on my body.

Echo and Morgen were not happy, either, and the exhaustion made the journey back down into Crossunder much more complicated than the first time. The lack of progress defeated us, and with one day left in the mission, I had no clue how we would catch a killer in this massive city.

My body hit the hay bed and cotton sheets like a puff of cloud, but I felt none of it. I floated off into a loud, uncomfortable snore, dreaming of nothing.

CHAPTER 10

INTO THE TIDE

"What happens if we don't catch him?" Echo stared at the pacing guard at the bottom of the bell tower. Her voice was quiet and numb.

We were back at the tower continuing our mission. Neither Morgen or I spoke, there was nothing to say. We all knew Baalthor might not even give us a second glance if we failed this mission. Biron himself may expel us all from the school.

Morgen leaned over and rested his head against her shoulder. "Don't think that far ahead."

"That far ahead? This is our last night." Her eyes narrowed on him and she pulled away from his touch. "What do you think is going to happen to us?"

He shrugged.

In the watchful night, we stared down at the men below and watched the city in all its nothingness. I had thought about him moving to a new area a few times, but it was also highly doubtful. This man had stayed consistent to this side because it accessed the water system and the direct path to the Isle.

I thought of the Isle.

The way the shore would bring cold fronts and the worst rains. People buried their gold to protect it when straw houses blew away.

Mother and father would cook meals for the hut-less dragons and welcome children into our stone home. If they could, they would have taken the world into their four walls.

Echo and I menaced the town folk in those days by climbing and jumping from buildings and statues or swimming out into the sea, only to need assistance getting back to shore when we went too far.

I stared at her.

She was lost, hanging over the edge of the railing on the other side of the tower. Not much else had been said since earlier in the night.

A shout called me to Morgen's side. Interest peaked; he ducked his head lower, still looking over and watching for more. I ducked with him, looking him over. "What happened?"

Waving me off, he listened. We both did.

But the clock tower was four stories high and everything said from below came back to us muffled.

He shook his head, defeated. "We have to go down there."

"No, we don't. You know they didn't find anything." Echo stayed slumped, not interested in this new development.

I crawled to her side and gripped her shoulders. "Snap out of this funk. We are going to catch a killer."

When I released her, I slid to the ladder and made my way to the ground. Looking back, neither of them had followed until a few minutes later. Echo came down first and then Morgen. Ducking behind another building and a stack of barrels, we avoided being caught by mere seconds.

Morgen signaled with his hands, pointing us to split in different directions. Echo shook her head and I motioned for her to accompany me. Morgen agreed to this with a wave of a hand and then disappeared around the corner of the closed tavern.

A couple of guards were huddled in the street down the road from the bell tower. Their weapons were drawn with tight fists clenching their hilts. Something had bothered them enough to put them on high alert. Echo leaned her back against the brick behind me, not giving it a glance of attention.

The guards whispered, eyes darting around to watch every few moments. I looked for a way to get closer, but Echo pulled me back, dragging me away from the scene somewhere with fewer eyes.

"What are you doing?" I jerked my hand from hers and stopped. Shadows were not moving and the wind was still. Echo's eyes widened, glistening in the light of the moon.

"Nala, I..." She started, but lost whatever thought disappeared with her mouth dropped open.

I gripped her shoulders again, this time with a more gentle touch, leaning over her with a downward gaze. "We will not fail."

"Nala, what if we do?"

"Then we will return to Biron and report the mission as a failure."

She dropped her look and turned it to the ground, but I didn't stop my thought.

"Then you will accompany me to Homecoming, wearing that gorgeous dress you selected."

That snapped her right back to me. "What?"

"And we will dance and party and celebrate—"

She said nothing.

I drew a breath. "Then—together—we will unenroll. Our parents will welcome us home and we will make a life for ourselves on the island. Because if there is no chance to end this semester with you by my side, then I do not want any of this."

"Nala," she cried.

"Echo, you are my best friend. There has never been a day that you haven't saved my ass or cared about how I felt. Every time I struggled, you picked me up and encouraged me. Without you, I wouldn't have made it through the Junior Paladin School."

Tears burned down her scales and I leaned closer. "Echo, I love you. I have always loved you."

Without hesitation, I stepped back and bowed at the waist, pulling one hand behind me. "Will you go to Homecoming with me?"

"Yes," she cried, pulling me back into her arms. "I cannot believe you waited so long to ask me."

With her head nuzzled against my chest, I laughed. "You have no idea how much courage I had to muster for this."

She stayed there in my arms a moment longer, quiet.

We were both startled at the sound of boots. Ducking into a crouched position, both ends of the alley opened onto a new road with guards. Between our search and Echo pulling me away, we had drifted more west than I would've liked to have stayed. Panicking under the constraint of time, I pulled open a back door and fled with Echo inside a closed building. The sounds of boots scuffing against the dirt ground passed and we breathed.

The door did not creak and we slipped back into the

alley, following behind the guard until we crossed the road and plunged into the southern sector of Crossroads. Echo tried to shout-whisper my name, slowing me down and making me turn to her again.

"We are running out of time. I think Morgen might have headed back to the sewer drain." She pointed down the road to the cool, gray tones splaying over the buildings. The sun was rising and we were out of time.

Another shout called out somewhere and I knew then someone had been killed.

"I cannot let him go free." Then, I sprinted for the ocean as she chased after me. My legs were longer and my pace faster, just as it had been when we were kids. Together, we sprinted to where the sand meets the sea, but this time, it wasn't to see who could swim out the furthest.

An aura danced on my tongue and the spark of magic stopped me. Echo felt it, too. She flinched back, looking for someone in the shadows of early dawn.

A muffled scream drew me back and I fell upon a trail of drops of blood. The ocean had been singing louder at this point. It crashed in waves along the sand and rock. The city was half a mile back up the small hill. But there, dressed in black, was a hooded figure with his hand outstretched ahead of him. When I rounded the scene, a human man with his eyes widened had a knife made of ice pressed against his throat.

Everything moved in seconds. The knife slid and his blood poured across his body as it collapsed, covered in the thin, white grain that shifted as he fell upon it. Crimson now covered the white beach where too much blood had already been spilled before.

I drew my sword. "Finally. This is the day you join your victims."

"Is it, Nala?" The hooded figure turned. The jacket he had been wearing was wrapped around his waist. When he turned, his leather armor peaked from behind the opening.

I laughed.

I wasn't sure why I was laughing, but it all made sense.

Echo whimpered like a scared little girl. I had never seen her so frightened. But I left her behind me and launched.

He had already drawn from his belt loop as I came down with my blade. They rang and the sound was carried along the beach. As he stepped forward, I slid back. The sand made it harder to move, but it also disadvantaged him. He moved slowly, shuffled with less grace and slipped his blade. When mine pierced, he shrieked and withdrew. I hadn't come close enough to do much damage, but now his blood met the sand.

I launched again. "If you think you will leave here alive, you are wrong."

"I've seen you fight. You're not impressive." He countered my blade and adjusted on his feet as he pressed in on me.

Echo hadn't moved an inch, still standing there frozen.

"That's not what Biron says." I counter his attempt at a blow, sliding down his blade and returning a combo of attacks that led him in a false direction. He moved left and I did, too. His blade came across my armor, but mine slid across his abdomen.

"Pathetic." I spat, but he laughed.

Gods, was he just crazy?

The ocean crashed further and the sand slid from beneath us. Water claimed our ankles and I fell forward. Even in my instability, I met his blade and we crashed into the water. It was chilled in the morning temperatures with my back pressed into the cold, wet sand and water enveloping most of us. He pressed down on my protective position, our blades struggling between us.

As the coast receded, I chucked a leg into his torso, flipping him onto his back. Our blades did not falter.

Echo was screaming our names and incoherent pleas.

The tide returned, weakening his grip as his face was submerged. I closed my eyes and pressed harder, avoiding the salted wave. My blade grew closer to his throat, but in the recession, the sand withdrew back and slid us further into the coast.

He spit the water in his nostrils as I slid from atop him. We both got from our knees to our feet. I slashed at his blade, water returning to our knees. When he released my edge and swung, I ducked. He splashed into the tide, and as it disappeared, I pounced.

Fumbling for a better grip, his eyes widened and I saw that genuine fear return to his eyes. The tide cried beneath the stars and as I raised my blade.

"Goodbye, Morgen."

Echo screamed and as we went under, I pierced him through the heart.

There hadn't been a chance to take a breath.

We had been pulled into the ocean and I danced beneath the surface, my hand retracting the blade from him. He stilled, bubbles escaping between his parted lips. Between my struggle and his sinking corpse, I heard her cries somewhere beyond.

My full plate armor weighed me down and each thrust and kick of a leg only got me so close. Each tide pulled me further from her and I ran out of time. When all my strength had fallen from my limbs, my eyes closed and I stilled.

Then she was, hands wrapped against my torso, pulling me to the surface. We both gasped and raced toward the shore. The tide had spit us out and we crawled into the dry sand, coughing and spitting up what was consumed.

She turned to the ocean, staring and waiting for him, but he did not come.

"He's gone."

The sounds of shouts and distant boots gathered above the hill where the road leads to the city. We both stood, gathering ourselves.

We had killed the Crossroads killer.

Then, my eyes fell upon the man: Morgen's last victim. There had been no proof of what had happened here, only two dragons standing over a body.

With their weapons raised, ten soldiers of the Church of Light surrounded us. I pulled Echo to my body, shivering from the water dripping off us.

"Stay where you are."

"No. No, you got it all wrong," I growled.

"It's over."

The sun broke the horizon and warmed my back. Its rays danced over each man as another shuffle came from above. Pointing down at the scene were five dark elves with bows and a man with his fancy, great ax at the ready. They did not flinch when the light hit them.

"Release them," the man called.

The guards did not move.

"Nala."

I looked up to the top of the hill.

"Run."

His men launched their arrows and reloaded a new set. The guards raised shields, faltering their pointed swords. I relinquished my blade to its sheath and my hand burned.

Each scale rippled in its place, moving and growing. The heirloom on my hand gleamed and I extended it into a dragon twice the size of Echo.

She smiled and gripped me back when I scooped her into my hand and launched into the sky. The men around us fell back and the Church of War attacked.

Within a few flaps, my wings glided and Echo climbed onto my back. Ripples of red and orange overtook the sky with the Kelti Forrest was just ahead.

The air was dry and cold. Together, we flew back in silence until I could smell it. Both of us turned to the sun. Somewhere distant to us was a puff of smoke turning the sky gray again. Romar's light peered around it.

I hurried forward harder, heading for the school. Echo stared into the sun.

Even as we passed the forest, it seemed unsettled. The whole world came alive this morning. The school grounds came up fast and a figure stood out front on the main lawn, waiting. My paws thudded into the grass and Biron screamed. "Go! Go now to Isle!"

Echo stilled and I pulled myself in to tuck and launch.

"They've attacked. The Church of Light landed two hours ago on a wide-scale attack. Go!"

The sky welcomed me again and Echo breathed with heavy, calculated breaths.

Sixty miles.

The smoke thickened just below the regular clouds. With the sun high enough in the sky now, the smoke covered its view and made it harder to navigate to the island. My body was weakening, the magic settling back down as I counted the seconds. I lowered just above the ocean's surface when the coast was fifteen miles away. A gasp escaped from Echo's throat.

Flames fed the sky ahead. Buildings that should have towered across the land were rubble. Boats from the mainland surrounded it and they were all doing it again.

My wings dipped, touching the water and throwing us sideways from land.

"What are you doing?" Echo cried.

I was avoiding crossfire from the boats.

The closer we flew, the more apparent it became that dragons were launching into the smoke above and striking down on the intruders. We fought back with all the power and force we had. I stayed out of the way, ducking into a clear, more minor coast. Just as I swooped down to land, the magic failed and threw us against the cliff of rocks.

My body bled somewhere, the cold liquid running against my scales; I lay there panting as the world spun from above me. If it wasn't for the muffled calling of my name, I felt I wouldn't have returned to my body.

"*Nala!*"

I jerked up straight, but no one was there. Echo was gone from where I remember seeing her. The ground shook enough to draw me to my knees.

Shaking, my hands warmed and a gold aura grew around me. Whatever wounds I had collected closed and I was ready to return home.

Rocks tumbled into the water as I climbed to the top. This part of the island had already been burnt and collapsed. The ground was covered in weapons, belongings, and the bodies of dragon-kind and Romar soldiers. I prayed as my feet caught air in a sprint.

Lord Baalthor, King and God of War, imbue me with your power and allow me to take us home. Let us purge these intruders from our land and bring back pride to our race.

Baalthor, protect me in all I am about to do.

I searched huts as I passed them, looking for survivors needing help. Most of the battle had moved to the northern coast, where I begged fate to allow my parents and their home to stand still. Echo was nowhere in my path.

"Nala!"

When I turned around to look for that voice, I saw that it was not there. I had heard it earlier on the coast, but it was unrecognizable. Now, it was so clear and so new. It had no emotion, but it screeched. The sound was more like a demand than a call.

Then I sprinted north towards my home, parents, and people.

Soldiers with swords raised knocked down children and burned houses as screams crackled through the air. I swung my sword at a soldier terrorizing a young dragonkin. He faltered and my blade pierced through. When he toppled over, I told the young woman to run away from there.

She wasted no time and disappeared behind a building. The ground crunched and I swung around to meet another soldier's blade. We danced and I pressed him forward. An ancient dragon swooped down from above and swiped a claw at anyone in the path ahead. My opponent turned to cry out for someone and I sliced him across the neck.

Burning beneath me, I ran forward and screamed for the young to run.

"Get out! Get out of your houses! Run for the south!"

Pulling rubble from across bodies, I checked for life along the way to the coast.

"Go!" I cried.

The world expanded at the top of the road and Echo was down in the middle, holding back two other men. They struggled against her sword and I watched as she stepped and slashed. Her entire body was light in movement. When the first man died, the second caught her in her recovery.

She screamed and I ran for her.

"ECHO!"

HOMECOMING

E cho cried as the sword slung her blood into the gravel. It dripped from her shoulder, painting her scales along the way. She did not straighten. With her head still dropped from the recoil, she laughed and then lunged. Her sword swung from behind her and struck one man's plate as the other advanced.

I slipped down the gravel hill, the taste of battle bringing my sword up and down on the other man. Echo's eyes widened, glossy when they met mine, but she continued and pushed him back as she could. He'd step and then she would follow with a swing, clashing blades with a piercing ring. Her chest heaved between them, tears falling to the ground. I don't think I had ever seen her so mad.

She straightened again, and beneath our feet, the island shook. Screams rung, and as her blade pierced, the man fell limp at her feet.

My blade collided with the other man and he heaved his own back. Echo was quiet behind me, but I was sure she was still there. I hadn't heard the sound of her feet or the sheathing of her weapon. My hands pulsed against the sword's hilt, glowing that red warmth. It spread across the blade, heating its tip. On my next blow, in Baalthor's name, the man collapsed.

Within wild breaths, my chest heaved up and down. The tip of my sword found an aperture in the gravel and waited.

"Are you alright?" I began to say, turning to find Echo with my eyes. But she was not at the distance I had left her. She was right upon me, blade raised, fury and sadness deep within her eyes. I hadn't had the time to bring my sword up and block hers, so when it came down on my chest, I bled and stumbled back across the man's body on the ground.

She didn't speak.

The words hesitated on my lips. Between widened eyes and a guttural groan, I slipped my leg back and raised my sword and elbows, waiting.

Shifting between her legs and readjusting her arms, she did not break the glance; she did not cower or cry anymore.

"Echo."

"Nala," she returned. She leapt across the body and swung down upon my blade with her own. I stepped back with each swing, blocking and turning when needed to avoid having to retaliate.

"Echo!" I cried. "What are you doing?"

"What needs to be done—" Her sword slid and she swung. When I stumbled forward against her false move, I realized I had never seen her in such capacity. These techniques were advanced, not ones we had learned at the college. She moved with a soldier's grace, I couldn't believe it.

"There's nothing left. I will be damned if I die, too." Her body pressed against mine, our swords entangled between. "My mother. My father. My little sister. Morgen."

I huffed, straining for air. "What are you talking about?"

"Dead. Nala. They are all dead. I cannot die, too. I can't. I have come too far. It will all be for nothing and I cannot let it all go for nothing."

I refused to hit her back. I refused. This was my best friend. I hadn't thought we'd grown this far apart. What about Homecoming? What about running away together? I finally dared to ask, and now I am, face to face with her. But this is not her. This is not Echo. This is not my best friend.

She huffed. "I cannot let you go, Nala. Not now–not when you know."

I stopped, taking several steps back and withdrawing from her sword. It startled her from the moment and she breathed, holding her blade frozen in front of her.

"You knew," I whispered.

She didn't blink. Her clothes rattled in the soft, calm wind. Even though the chill was enough to cause a shiver, it didn't break us from that look—that betrayal.

I thought about it. The late nights studying with Morgen instead of hanging out with me. All those times he was there by her side. I hadn't stopped to consider, didn't think to worry. I was scared he had been hurting her or troubling her in ways that maybe she was already troubled.

My friend.

I hadn't really known my friend for a few semesters now. How long have they been plotting?

"Why?"

"You wouldn't even begin to understand. Even if I spent countless hours explaining it to you. He made these promises... This guarantee."

"You're right; I wouldn't understand." I stiffened, staring at her empty face now cold and hostile. "So which was the lie, me or him?"

"Both."

"Both." I scoffed. "So this is it. Here I am, concerned for your safety, worried about your death. Here I am, ready to leave it all for a liar. *You knew* what he was doing to our home."

She widened her jaw, her fangs slipping from her upper lip. "This is not our home."

I tightened my grip on the blade.

"It was never our home. The elders were never going to fight to get our land back. Morgen promised he could get the dragons off the Isle—" she stuttered, her eyes darting around and then back to me. "I just never knew how. This ploy, I didn't know he was antagonizing for an attack. I didn't see the fury he wished upon us. I'm sorry."

"You stupid girl." I shook my head.

She lowered her sword. "I messed up, Nala. When I realized he was killing those people, I was already in a deep hole. There was no backing away without him targeting me. I wouldn't be his competition. And then we started hunting him. He said if you ever found out, you would kill him and then me. I hoped…"

She stepped forward and I let her. "I hoped you would find out and kill him. Because I loved you. I loved you and I liked him, I wanted to make it all work."

I softened my grip, my shoulders dropping.

"Echo." I sighed.

"Now that you know, it's over. I cannot have you tell them I was a part of this. It would tarnish my family's name."

"Echo, Biron will investigate. I cannot lie to him or Baalthor."

She sniffled and we stood there for a quiet moment.

"Then I am sorry, Nala." Her sword rose and her eyes

narrowed. Glinting in the flames, the edge was ready to burn into my scales. My fingers slipped down along the leather bind of my own, tightening. It spun along my palm, and as I dodged, I launched, the tip piercing through the softness of her chest. With widened eyes, her blade fell between us. She drew her hands to the wound, melting to her knees and then onto her back. I sank to her side, watching the tears gather, the pain washing out her beautiful face.

There, in my young years, I had believed I had killed my soulmate. That young and tireless infatuation I had for her slipped away between her consciousness and death. I placed a hand on her head, stroking it softly. "You stupid girl. Didn't anyone ever tell you not to fall in love?"

She choked, blood gathering in her throat. "I didn't love him."

"I know."

Her eyes gathered that sadness again when she recognized what I meant, and just as something came to her tongue, she was gone. That light I had always seen inside her vanished. I draped across her body and wailed. I was so angry, so struck by the hurt, but I wailed for my best friend and the loss it brought to my heart.

She was gone; maybe she had been gone awhile. I didn't want to see it. My best friend was scheming, lying, and choosing to become someone so unrecognizable.

Then I was numb. Sitting up from her blood-soaked body, I stared at it all gathered in my hands and across my scales. My wounds were covered now, by whose blood was unknown.

I would go on now.

Standing, I pulled myself and my sword from the ground, my head still bowed to her. Then, I turned to search for the rest of the chaos plaguing the island. I wasn't sure where everyone had gone; this side was so quiet and dead. The darkness shadowed buildings that were only smoke and ash now as time snuffed out the fire. There weren't many bodies, but the ones that did lay still, I recognized as neighbors and old souls that had seen the worst days of our kind. They will never know the world I plan to create.

Paladin of War.

I was not scared to graduate now. I would do whatever was necessary to fix this.

A spark wisped into a figure, tall and human; he towered nearly seven feet and was startled from his stance. With green, raging eyes, his lip curled, his body bending down and withdrawing the first thrown-about sword on the ground to place inside his grasp.

He wore no church on his battered clothes, the faded tan cloth dripping over his malnourished form. It was as if he had appeared from thin air and snuck upon this battle. As he charged, I raised my blade, preparing, but his figure blinked. His speed changed as if he was no longer material before me; he wasn't a few feet away, but a few inches and his blade was gone.

No, not gone.

It burned.

His human face contorted into a devilish smile and he let go of the hilt. I gripped it, pulling together my strength to withdraw it from my abdomen, but stumbling back as I dropped, he laughed. "You will never rid me, Nala."

Then he was gone in a blink and I was staring helplessly into the night sky, the gravel collecting me like the rest of my laid-out kind.

Death was lingering near; I could feel him creeping up my spine. I should've prayed, but didn't; my thoughts felt bare. The stars seemed brighter tonight; I hadn't even considered how the world must've been watching. What will happen now that I will be gone?

My chest rattled in a rough and blood sputtered over the edge of my lips.

What will my parents say when they find out I have failed them?

My hands were too heavy now; they dropped to my side, my head slouching over to see the body across the way. Echo was still. Still dead. Soon, I would be, too.

Soon.

My eyelids closed and I imagined I could still see the stars in that pitch-black darkness.

Until I was gone.

CHAPTER 12

DESTINY IS DEAD

I had forgotten what time felt like. The elven man before me didn't move and the orc behind me wouldn't stop screaming. Somehow, I thought it had only been minutes since I had joined this line of people, but if that was so, how were there already so many behind me?

Soggy eyes and horrified faces gathered and gathered, but the line did not move. Those ahead of me turned lifeless and unresponsive. I waved a hand before the man's face and he didn't even blink.

No one sat on the throne at the front of the line; this empty, wall-less room just filled and stretched, but did not move. I couldn't feel any part of my body. My heart was not beating, my chest did not rise, and that wound, the one with all the blood, was gone.

I was dead.

All of these people were dead.

Was this the afterlife? A bad dream?

Peace had never felt so good. It was all I could feel. This unwavering calm washed over every moment I've ever had and nothing hurt anymore. I thought of my parents and siblings, but knew they would be all right. Dying in honor is what I was meant to do. This was my destiny, after all.

Something tugged at my chest. It dragged my shoulders forward and rolled across my body, the only sensation I had felt since opening my eyes here. The walls ran away, sucking me forward somewhere golden and bright. A castle of mechanics, a clockman on his throne, and another clockman beside him. Identical. Fifty feet tall.

They talked in tongues, a foreign but familiar language, the one of the Gods.

No one ever saw the Gods in their whole form; they'd be lucky to see them, but here I was before the God of Time, chosen for a reason unbeknownst to me.

When his eyes slid to mine, the two pits of endless time, I bowed low, dropping to my knees before the creatures.

"I don't understand." My voice echoes the vaulted room, the ceiling stretching nearly a hundred feet above.

"What do you not understand?" The clockman beside the throne spoke.

I straightened, still pressing my knees into the marble. "Why am I here? Am I not dead?"

The two beings exchanged glances but said nothing.

My throat bobbed as I swallowed. "I am dead, aren't I?"

"Yes." The one on the throne said. The clock above his head ticked in contemplation and stopped when the second hand met the twelve. "You are dead."

The other man turned to him, his voice slow and monotonous. "Do you understand?"

He nods.

"But I don't. If I am dead, why am I here? Do I not get an afterlife? A place to rest? Have I not earned it?"

They both turned, heads creaking and looking back at me. Two clocks, one above each of their heads, ticked until it met the twelve again.

"I see."

"You understand."

"I do."

The replica of the clock man's body began to wisp. Edges of metal flaking into sparks and turning into dust. He nodded to me. "Goodbye for now, Nala Delvimir."

Then, I was alone with the man on the throne.

"Do you know who I am?"

"The God of Time," I said.

He nodded. "Time is such a precise thing. In the face of death, justice is the final testament that transcends mortal reality, ensuring fairness prevails even in your last breath. However, you did not get fairness in your death."

"What do you mean?"

He pauses. "You will one day understand, but your mortal mind is too young now."

"What now, then?"

"Now you will go home. This will feel simple and forgotten. When you are ready, it will all make sense one day."

"Alive?" My eyes water.

"Alive. Your destiny is not dead yet."

His hand outstretched. Weaves of strings are pulled from between the universe and me, untangling, reuniting, and bending back into a perfect web. They wrap around my body, flood into my soul, and in a spark, I gasp into a breath, sitting up from the cold gravel beneath the night sky. The sword was still resting between my intestines; its silver-winged hilt glossed in blood. I withdrew it from my body, pulling it into my hand, and the wound sealed.

"You pique my interest a little more daily, Nala." Baalthor towers forward, red eyes glowing in rage. "But I do believe my champion is ready now?"

My eyes widened and I adjusted the hilt, nodding to him. "Yes, sir."

"Then let's rise."

CHAPTER 13

CHAMPION OF WAR

Baalthor lit the Church of Light ships on fire, igniting the very essence of their being and sending the people crashing down into the freezing waters. The ancient dragons of the Isle pulled together and eradicated the mainland threat. Then, we started pulling young and helpless survivors from collapsed and burning homes.

The Isle was destroyed, but we were not. As a people, we stood united and kept our homes. Baalthor's followers stood in awe, having never seen the deity in material form. It was a message and the dawning of a new era.

We would not bow down to our enemy.

We will not be destroyed.

EPILOGUE
GLASS CASTLES

THE BOOK OF LAW

Gold-foiled letters gleam beneath the touch of my padded claws and I stoke its length along the leather cover.

It burns.

With anger.

With worry.

With justice.

He asked me who I was and I had no idea what to tell him. That may be how it is. When you are presented with the scope of your life, how do you sum it up into a single word—or choice? But now it is so clear. That is burning. It is not from the book, but my will and power buzzing at the edge of my clawed fingers—the power of a God.

Dragonkind has gone with injustice for too long. Maybe Aeo knows the spark he stirred inside me. But we will no longer wait for the fight to come to us. We will no longer be kicked from homes, cities, mountains, or isles.

I parted the pages and slipped the arcane symbols

between my thoughts. They drifted beneath the surface deep within and I felt the power buzz.

Divinity.

The book still calls when I place it on the armrest of my throne to move toward the city below the glass castle. It wasn't as grand as the translucent kingdom I stand in, but it was blocks of order and lines of soul. Beings of lawful chaos wait for me. The sky churns in oranges and red in specks of stardust and clouds. It dances and webs all the secrets of the new world below it and I wonder what will come.

There is a mortal out there—one like I once was—someone willing to pray and sacrifice for a speck of power and hope.

A Champion of Law.

Even when I squint, I still cannot see past the veil onto the mortal plane where the souls bow to their knees and beg. But if I listen, my eyes closed and my thoughts quiet, I can hear their cries.

This is only the beginning.

Isn't that right, Baalthor?

The glass door creaked on its hinges as he pried it open and strolled inside. His hands are tucked neatly behind his back and his eyes radiate a light, airy wonder. Even with all the glass surrounding the two of us now, his adorned black and red armor shines far greater than anything. Clean, neat, and polished against his half-draconic form.

"Nala."

"Baalthor," I return.

He smirks and I do not bow.

TO BETRAY A GOD

PANTHEON

NALA

The tip of his claws click on the glass beneath him, meeting me in the middle of the room. With his head tilted, he cranes his neck, and I raise a brow. The Book of Law sits where I left it, and he takes in its sight. "Is it everything you wanted?"

It presses into my spine, the power, from behind me. As if it had eyes, it peels them open to look. And although it has none, I can feel it staring, waiting, wanting to know everything. Refusing to turn and acknowledge what it seeks, I straighten and smile. "Yes, yes, it is."

"Right." A fang slips between his lips with a cocky little smirk. "And what about Haven?"

"Haven?"

Slumping into a chair, he throws his feet over the edge, his half-draconic form slouching between the armrests. "She was given Asgard—an upper-orbit plane. At this point, by the bylaws, she has to remain chaotic neutral, which makes her a traitor to our side."

"I don't think she is planning that." My hands break into a cold sweat.

He raises a brow. "Really? Do you know something I don't?"

"I know she's a loyal person."

"Ha." He scoffs. "Loyal? Was she very loyal to Romar?"

There is nothing else I can say to argue that point. She didn't stay very loyal to Romar.

"I want to know where she lies, when and if she is lying."

"Why? What are you planning?"

Dropping his features into a cold look, he drew his eyes to mine. "The plan has not changed."

"We are taking everything."

Acknowledgments

The biggest thank you goes to my in-laws. Both the Brockway's and the Clark's. I am incredibly privileged to have you all as my village, both in my journey as a mother and academically. Nothing I would do would be possible without you all. Thank you for being here and accepting me in all that I am.

Taylor & Charles, my beautiful partners, I could not imagine any of this being a possibility without the stories we create and the people we play as in our table-top RPGs. Thank you for helping me write some crazy stories.

To my besties, Chey, Lancey, and Wonder, you three encourage me on a daily basis to give the world my one hundred and ten percent. Everything I do, I do in your encouragement and love. I could never ask for a better group of people to be at my side.

My friends, those of you who have followed me and known me since I was a child, those of you who supported me through the worst and best years of my life, thank you for being here. Thank you for never giving up on me and being proud of my growth.

To Booktok and Bookstagram, y'all are crazy amazing with

hyping me up and supporting my pages and books. My success comes from your love and compassion. Thank you.

To S & R, always my admirers and muses, thank you for reminding me of my imagination. My love for you is eternal.

Finally, a big thank you for the crazy mistakes I've made in friends. You all taught me to stop trusting so easily, and now that you've shoved the knife in my back too many times, my skin is thicker and I am better at selecting who has a place in my circle. You taught me an important lesson, and because of that, this story hits a little harder. I hope you read it and are ready to see what Nala becomes because her journey is far from over.

ALSO BY SARALYN EVERHART

Pantheon Series:

<u>BOOK ONE: HAVEN: Book of Knowledge</u>

<u>BOOK TWO: PANTHEON: Book of Deceit</u> estimated release in 2025

<u>Anthology Short Story</u>: **Blades For Hire: BURN** summer 2024

Corruption Series:

BOOK ONE: Wishing For Corruption December 7th 2024

GOODREADS

AMAZON AUTHOR PAGE

INSTAGRAM: @tomeofchaos

FACEBOOK: Author Saralyn Everhart

TIKTOK: @s.everhartauthor

About the Author

I was born in Paducah, Kentucky. I've spent most of my life in the western part of the state. But that didn't stop me from enjoying new places. I'd travel into worlds from my imagination and write stories from the places I could see. As it says in my birth chart, being a Pisces sun allows me to live in a chaotic plane of the divine that is not at all material. Since I could hold a pencil, I've written short stories in handcrafted staple-bound notebook paper books. Although there was a wide variety of short stories, the majority had two things in common: fantasy fiction and unicorns. I stuck with the fantasy theme. I don't know if you'll soon see me writing about unicorns.

I knew I'd never publish a book. My dyslexia made writing difficult as a child, and I never thought I would learn to get around it.

At 18, I began writing stories again as tabletop RPGs. Then, my fiancé brought the world of Pantheon to life, and after nearly four years of campaigning, I am sharing what we created together.

Although my chaotic plane of the divine doesn't just end with fantasy worlds and original characters, my unconventional family consists of two chaos beans (children) who bring out the magic in imagination. And as a stay-at-home mom of two under two, our days are full of it.